# Praise for
# *Rattle of Want*

Short stories are one of the purest forms of storytelling. Luckily for us, Gay Degani is a master at it.

~ Robert Swartwood, *USA Today* bestselling author of *New Avalon*

Short, bittersweet stories from a writer who knows just what makes us tick. Some are heart-stopping, some heart-breaking, but all these stories will make your world wider.

~ Sarah Hilary, author of the *Someone Else's Skin* and *No Other Darkness*

*Rattle of Want* is a narrative road trip across America, driven by memorable characters and prose with muscle. Degani is a consummate storyteller and a virtuosa of short fiction.

~ Christopher Allen, 2015 winner of *Ginosoko Literary Journal's* Flash Fiction

*Rattle of Want* ranges from brilliant brief experiments (such as *Abbreviated Glossary* and *Appendages*) to a novella-in-flash (*The Old Road*) for the canon in that new genre. Altogether these stories mine the wants and desires in the breakups of families, rebellions of youth, and occasional ascents of the spirit. Often they beautifully, and simply, nail a place, as in *Small Town* (a perfect evocation of the title), report an impending explosion, as in *Kindling* (a quintessential flash), or capture a character (if you haven't met *Blusterfuck* ... do so at your own peril). Few writers can do all that Gay Degani does.

~ Robert Shapard, editor of *Flash Fiction International: Very Short Stories from Around the World*

If you think of stories as noises, then Gay Degani will sometimes have you clamping your ears and other times leaning forward to soak every detail in. She pairs the ugly, imperfect, bumbling pieces of ourselves with the pure, beautiful parts of our souls.

~ Tara Laskowski, author of *Modern Manners for Your Inner Demons* and *Bystanders*

Award-winning author, Gay Degani, kills it again with this new collection. By turns smart, tender, dark, and always compelling, Degani gives us life in all its skewed realities and does so with finesse and vigor. This book is a knockout.

~ Kathy Fish, author of *Together We Can Bury It*

Each story in *Rattle of Want* made me flinch. A gun fired at the starting line, packed with either live ammunition, sex dream confetti, love or loss flash of party powder, or sometimes just a beautiful song, the likes of which you'll never hear again this pure.

~ Bud Smith, author of *F 250, Tollbooth* and *I'm From Electric Peak*

# Rattle of Want

### Gay Degani

**PURE SLUSH BOOKS**
Adelaide, Australia

**PURE
SLUSH
BOOKS**

ISBN: 978-1-925101-67-6

Pure Slush Books
4 Warburton Street
Magill SA 5072
Australia

Email: edpureslush@live.com.au
Website: http://pureslush.webs.com
Pure Slush Store: http://pureslush.webs.com/store.htm

Cover photograph © Tim Van Damme
Cover design by Matt Potter

Also available as an eBook
ISBN: 978-1-925101-68-3

For Tim,

without a doubt!

# Also by Gay Degani

What Came Before (2014)

Pomegranate Stories (2010)

# Contents

# Abbreviated Glossary

Want: I slide my naked leg between his thighs. Dev is trying a case tomorrow. He's tired, but he owes me his touch, and I know exactly how to use my tongue.

Pact: His lips disappear between his teeth when I break the news. He says he's not ready – no diapers for him – but I know he is. I'll do the hard part. I promise.

Hope: My fingers knead the curve of my belly. Dev slips an arm around my waist and grins at his boss. Proud papa.

Thrill: Dev can't keep his hands off me, calls me "sexy mama," but when he's not around, I fret. Eight months along and my bump so small.

Rift: Skull bones don't always fuse together, the doctor tells me. I call Dev, but he's in court, won't request a recess, even when I beg. The hard part, I see, will be losing both.

# Appendages

A man born with no arms and no legs, all torso and head, and one two-toed foot, jumped into a swimming pool and used his body to undulate to the surface. On a swath of country club grass, he sunk a putt and later, spun a hula-hoop around his neck. At age ten, he tried to drown himself in the bathtub. He slipped under the water and turned face down. He said his body and mind were willing, but his heart was not.

The Los Angeles basin is often referred to as a desert. When parrots first appeared in Pasadena, the flocks were sparse. Now they converge in the oaks at dusk all clatter and turbulence, wheeling through dusky orange skies. The story goes that a pet store burned to the ground in 1959 and while most of the animals perished, the parrots took wing.

Tesla – the company not the man – has introduced a luxury electric car, the Model X. Its rear doors open and fold over the top. They call them falcon-wings. The DeLorean with its stainless steel shell and similar gull-wing styling was featured in the movie *Back to the Future* thirty years ago, a futurist hot-rod cast as time machine. Both vehicles were designed to move through space – and epochs – with distinct chasses, motors, and extraneous wings.

Research reveals that being born without arms and legs is rare. The disorder called "tetra-amelia syndrome" is caused by a mutation in the WNT3 gene. It is quite different from "quadriplegia" or "tetraplegia" — these the result of disease or more frequently, injury. Actor Christopher Reeve who lost the use of his arms and legs after being thrown from a horse is perhaps the most famous victim of spinal-cord fracture.

Biologists have been studying bird migration in connection with global warming. Apparently, many species are moving away from the equator to cooler climes at the rate of fifteen feet per day. The Audubon Society states that birds are the most adaptable of wildlife.

Leonardo da Vinci, obsessed with the idea that man could fly, filled his notebooks with detailed drawings of birds, the structure of their wings, the shape of their tails. From these studies, he constructed an apparatus of light wood, gauze, and feathers, hoping his assistant could leap from a cliff and soar. He did not. Eventually Leonardo invented both the helicopter and the parachute.

As a child, the armless-legless man was given a plastic prosthesis fitted to his shoulders. Experts claimed it would create the illusion of arms as well as increase his ability to function. The boy who had already taught himself to ride a skateboard on his belly and play ball with his head found the artificial appendages clumsy. He soon abandoned them.

Parrots are known for bright plumage and the ability to mimic human speech. They tend toward monogamous breeding, the males courting their mates with a "parade-like walk" and a blaze in the eye.

In *Back to the Future*, teenager Marty McFly jumps into Emmett Brown's DeLorean and tumbles into 1955 at the moment his parents are about to meet. To bring and keep them together, Marty teaches his father to stand up for himself.

Before Christopher Reeve had to rely on mechanical breathing and a wheel chair, he starred in the 1978 movie, *Superman*, in which he saves the life of Lois Lane by flying around the earth so fast, he manages to reverse time.

Da Vinci began his painting, "Mona Lisa," around 1503, and it is believed it took him several years to complete. There is speculation about the woman who sat for him, who she was, and why her smile is so enigmatic. Perhaps she was only in love?

Nick Vujicic, the man born without limbs, the one who sought to end his life in the bathtub at age 10, was married in 2012. A recent television show ended with a video of him waltzing with his bride atop his electric wheelchair. They were expecting a baby.

# Beyond the Curve

Three months after Allen Winter's bicycle became a tangle of aluminum on Huntington Drive, his widow Carol moved into a small cottage along the Arroyo. The new property was tucked into a curve of the road, the narrow front yard closed off by white oleander and a six-foot iron fence. The path leading to the front door, visible at the gate, soon became invisible because, like the street, it too was curved.

An alley ran along her walled-in backyard where an automatic gate spanned the driveway. She never left her car until the garage door slid down behind her.

In the cottage, she'd hung no pictures, none of Allen and none of their son. No art, although Carol herself was an artist. Jewelry. Stones and magnets.

But six months after Allen's death, she finally began to breathe. She felt no pressing want or need, just a vague niggle that maybe she'd do something about the barren walls today.

Later in the shower, hot water streaming down her body, she saw Allen beyond the misty glass as if he were caught inside an impressionist painting. Bright red latex, yellow striping, helmet in one hand, a leg swung over his bike, each color blurred. She turned away, twisted a knob, flinched as cold water splashed her breasts, her stomach, the tops of her legs.

Thoughts of hanging pictures evaporated with the steam. Carol dried off, threw on sweats and rubbing her arms, began to pace through the barren cottage, shivering. In the kitchen, she dug for decaf in the freezer. Rinsed the coffee pot. Reached for the grinder. A shout jolted her, dried her throat. Then a bellow, louder, longer. Coming from somewhere in her front yard.

She crept through the shadowed dining area and into the entry. Pulled aside the linen curtain. Sycamores, a bit of sky, no one in view.

The word "Help!" made her unbolt and swing open the door. Bright light washed across the polished oak floors, followed by the sweet smell of eucalyptus.

She ventured onto the brick path, moving slowly, tentatively, to where it curved toward the street. Dangling from her six-foot fence was a red-haired, red-faced boy, his flannel shirt snagged on an iron finial. He was younger than her son, maybe 15 or so, holding onto the metal posts, twisting up his knees to keep his baggy pants from slipping off his hips.

"Hey!" she shouted. "You're trespassing."

"Dude, I just wanna sell you a magazine."

"That's why I keep the gate locked."

"I thought it was stuck. Dude, nobody locks his front – Oh! Shit!"

His pants slid toward his naked feet, taking Spiderman boxers – Spiderman! – with them. The boy curled his legs upward and groaned.

She pivoted away, hiding an unbidden smile.

"Not funny," the kid said. "Can't you do something?"

She crossed the lawn toward him. A worn pamphlet and a receipt pad rested on the grass and on the other side of the fence lay Nikes and tube socks. "Why'd you take off your shoes?"

"Didn't wanna rip 'em. Don't look! Just hand me those boxers."

Averting her face, she leaned down, picked up the underwear. He nabbed them from her and pushed against her arm with his foot. She stumbled backward and he yelped, "Sorry, dude."

"What if we both hold them, so you can at least get your leg in?" she asked.

"Okay, but don't look." He held them out. She grasped one side of the waistband, he the other. Keeping her eyes shut, she felt him struggle to get a foot in. Then with the sharp sound of fabric ripping, he bumped against her and landed on the grass with a thump.

Glimpsing the white back under his torn flannel shirt, she laughed.

"Go ahead," he said. "Make fun of me. Just buy a magazine, okay?"

"I don't read magazines."

He sat on his butt, his legs spread. "You gotta read *People*. Everybody reads *People*. How're you gonna know what's going on in the world?"

"I don't think *People* —"

"I got others. I got a whole speech. I memorized it. You got something better to do?"

She should send this pushy boy packing. He would go, she thought, if she explained about Allen. Allen. How he loved to ride that damn bike. She stared through the iron gate into the empty street.

When she slowly turned back, eyes wet, the kid stood in his bare feet, his baggy shorts now resting on his hips, Spiderman underwear peeping out, the magazine pamphlet unfurled in his hand, his face eager. She shook her head and strode away, heart squeezing and unsqueezing, up the path.

Broken light sifted through the sycamores, caressed her taut face, slow-danced against the rosy brick. She halted, staring into the open door of the cottage where an empty interior waited. Outside, the scent of eucalyptus again.

Did she really have anything better to do?

She would need a hammer and nails. She would start there in the entry – on that first wall that now looked more silver than gray – with a picture of all three of them, Allen, Jimmie, and herself. And then she'd hang the rest.

But first, she turned back to the boy, his red hair glinting in the sun, as he watched her. The oleanders nodded behind him.

She waved. "I'll take one or two of those magazines. Let me get my wallet."

He grinned. "Duuuude!"

# Small Town

Seen from the air, Tauton, population 113, is shaped like a crucifix. One gravel road connects east and west to the rest of the world while the other gravel road becomes "Main Street" for a quick five minutes before continuing nineteen miles south through soybeans to Interstate-80.

The school, a modest brick building separated from weedy playing fields by a dirt parking lot, spreads along the top of the "†". Flanking the trunk of the cross are a half dozen clapboard houses, a post office/gas station, a cornfield, a big stone house, four more homes, a creek bridge, two small grocery stores, and a dairy farm.

One would think there would be at least one chapel, perhaps in the grassy field on the north side of the bridge, where a forest of American hornbeam stretches wide its branches, but all the churches are in neighboring towns, the Lutheran in Weaver, the Catholic in Mahaska, a Methodist just over the county line in Ionia.

On Sunday mornings, cars and trucks exit Tauton in all directions. However, not everyone feels the need to worship with others. Some families gather in living rooms to read their Bibles while the unrepentant congregate in front of Bohlander's grocery with cigarettes and whiskey-laced coffee. This is where Mr. Flood tips back his chair to lecture on the depravity of the world and the sundry reasons he left Boston to live in a big stone house next to a cornfield in Iowa.

Tauton is the kind of place where the unthinkable never happens, but then it does. Despite the dedication of community leaders and hard-working teachers, the vigilance of county deputies, the outsized civic pride of residents, Tallie McEnroe, age 16, goes missing on a Sunday morning in July.

The eldest of nine children, Tallie asks her parents if she can skip church because of a migraine. Mostly she's hung over from drinking in Mahaska the night before, using a phony ID forged by her boyfriend, and she's not in the mood to hold squirmy children on her lap. Her mother, who knows the girl came in at two in the morning, will hear none of it, but to everyone's surprise, the father says it's okay, give the girl a break, let her stay home this once.

A short while after the McEnroe's old Suburban rattles out of town, the post-mistress, on her way to Mass, backs her Chevy onto Main Street and spies the girl sauntering through the cornfield next to the old stone house.

Later when the county sheriff takes her official statement, he asks, "What do you mean by 'sauntering?' Do you mean aimlessly wandering around or like she was waiting for someone?" The post-mistress asserts she has no idea.

During his interview with the sheriff, Mr. Flood who lives in the stone house, reports hearing a rifle shot sometime during the afternoon. Although hunting season hasn't started yet, it's not unusual for someone to be out poaching. No one else remembers a gunshot.

The sheriff interrogates Tallie's boyfriend as well as a hitchhiker seen on Route 10, the disreputable Sloane brothers who live five miles out in a ramshackle farmhouse, and a crazed escapee from a mental hospital downstate, but there's no evidence to arrest any of them, let alone indict. No other lurking strangers are seen. No rifle discovered. No trace of the girl.

Her teachers tell reporters from as far away as Iowa City that Tallie is a good student, sullen at times, but a good girl with a bright future. The grocer, Mr. Bohlander, says she's a wiz at math. She helps him keep the books. When the post-mistress is asked again and again about what she saw, her answer never varies, "She was sauntering in the corn." The girl's boyfriend weeps. No one calls *60 Minutes.*

Tallie's mother barely speaks to anyone about her daughter, barely looks up when spoken to, but late at night in bed, stiffly turned to the wall, she berates her husband for his uncharacteristic permissiveness on the morning the girl disappeared.

To comfort his distraught wife, Tallie's father threatens to take the law into his own hands. He sends letters to police stations around the country. The post-mistress sells him stamps, sees the addresses, and shares this bit of information with the grocer when she picks up her eggs and laundry detergent. The neighbor, Mr. Flood, invites him over for a calming brandy. A conclusion is eventually reached that the girl has run away. Her father protests that not enough has been done, but his efforts, with time, cease.

In the seven years since Tallie McEnroe vanished, her parents have divorced, mother and children moving to Texas to live with relatives. The father stays in their unkempt house, drinking cheap bourbon, making duck decoys to sell on the Internet. He and Mr. Flood are friends now, smoking cigarettes and playing cards on Mr. Flood's screened-in front porch. They eat dinner together and watch T.V. Some people think this friendship is odd, Mr. Flood still considered a bombastic heathen. Those who are born-again whisper the word "gay." The post-mistress refers to Mr. McEnroe as "be-grieved."

Other than her defense of the father, the post-mistress never speaks of the girl anymore. She's afraid it will slip out of her mouth that she sometimes sees Tallie in the cornfield near her house or standing in the window of Mr. Flood's bedroom. She tells herself it's a trick of the light, a figment brought on by guilt that she was the last person to see the girl alive, that she needs to resurrect her, believe she isn't dead. Besides, the post-mistress is soon to retire, a widow getting older and blinder, prone to catching non-things out of the corner of her eye. Better she believe the girl is living in California untouched.

# Monsoon

Somewhere between Fountain Valley and Phoenix, I promise Rag and Mop everything two little girls might want: a glass dome under the big dipper, turquoise water, two regular Cokes from the Coke machine. What two little girls would want, that is, who are locked in a speeding car with a crazy man and a crazy woman. "If you're good," I tell them. "If you keep quiet." Rag is Regina, Mop is Margaret. The crazy man is Leo. The crazy woman is me.

The girls act like twins, look like twins, same nose, same hair – Leo's thick mat – same bony frame. Twelve months apart. Rag is the oldest, six, bossy, artistic. Mop, younger, pliant, funny. They are squealing like the brakes of a skidding car, and if they're not careful, I'll have to ask Leo to find a CVS in Blythe. The girls are asthmatic. I only brought one puffer.

Leo leans forward in the driver's seat, hands wrapped around the steering wheel like he's gripping my shoulders, digging in fingers. He likes to mine for pain.

The Suites Hotel in Phoenix is fake 80's opulent. Leo pulls under the portico and leaves the car running. Both girls want to go with him to register. He tells them no. I notice a dark blot of sweat on the back of his t-shirt as he yanks open the hotel's glass door with its palm tree decal. He disappears into the lobby.

I roll down my window. It's hot. Humid. Lightning cracks over Saddleback. It's going to rain. Monsoon season in Arizona.

"Mommy," says Mop, leaning into that small split between my seat and Leo's. Because the sun is buried in clouds, her face appears blue-gray.

"Mommy." Rag crowds in front of her sister. "Where's the sky dome?"

"What *is* a dome anyway?" asks Mop.

It isn't what you'd find in a church. Nothing like an Italian Duomo. The dome is long, rounded, a bullet of glass. The night, bleached gray from city lights, comes through with none of the promised stars. Under the dome is a kidney-shaped pool, the turquoise tiles encrusted with calcium. White plastic chairs, the kind you buy at Home Depot for $7.99 each, are scattered around the stained cement. I'm wearing the same sweaty shorts and top I've worn all day. The girls have on their bikinis, Rag in blue, Mop in shocking pink. They talk about sharks. They haven't gotten into the water yet.

Leo's gone to find a drugstore although neither girl is having trouble breathing yet. I didn't ask him to go. He just took off, taking the old inhaler with him. Tomorrow we're going up to the ranch, twenty-six miles from any town, no phone service. What else he'll do, I don't know. I don't want to think about quarters dropping into slots, long distant ringing, someone else's caressing voice.

The girls whisper and shove each other at the shallow end and though I can't hear them, I know what's going on: Rag conning Mop to jump in first.

"Is the water cold?" My raised voice sounds metallic in all this vaulted space.

"We don't know," says Rag.

"You better find out before Daddy gets back with Mickey D's."

I have no idea if Leo will remember to bring food. If Leo will even come back.

My thoughts drift to last night. I didn't want to go to the fundraiser. Didn't want to find a babysitter, an outfit that fits, nylons. And we were leaving on this trip, for Pete's sake. But the museum bought one of Leo's metal sculptures, the copper box, lidded in silver, grommeted in bronze. It's a good thing for his career. For him. For us. I had no choice.

There goes Mop — she can't resist her big sister — plunging down the steps into the water. Splashing. Shrieking. Rag follows. High decibel screams, high octane squeals.

Last night when Leo stood with that girl, thunder tore through me. Chemistry between two people is palpable. Like ozonic air before a storm. You can't see it, but your nose prickles, your skin tingles. You know it's there. I look down at my hands. They're shaking.

I was surprised she was so young. No more than 18, I'm sure. Leo isn't a good dancer, but she made him look as if he was, matching her step to his, tilting her body toward him, tapping her shoulder against his arm. Then him, taking her hand, spinning her around, watching her as if she were made of gold.

Silver bolts web the Phoenix sky. Thunder rattles. The rain comes hard and fast. I look at the glass in the dome and wonder if the putty will hold or if the heat of the desert sun has dried it up, crackled it with fissures.

The girls race across the deck. Dripping water. Mop slips, but Rag grabs her arm in time to keep her from falling. They rush around me, grab my arms, flop into my lap, and I realize I've forgotten to bring towels.

25

Sometime around 3 A.M, the storm quiets, and I wake. I've fallen asleep on the foldout couch with the girls. It's dark in the suite's living room, the blackout drapes shut tight. I move carefully from under Rag's arm and tiptoe into the bedroom.

Leo snores on top of the bed, his clothes still on. I step closer. Lean down. Hiss the word, "Asshole."

He doesn't wake up.



Leo comes out of the shower this morning pretending nothing is wrong. He must think if he gets on with it, his crazyjealouswife will get over it. For the sake of the girls I pretend I do, but I can't forget. When the music at the museum gala stopped, when the deejay's voice echoed over the mike he needed a break, Leo and that girl stood alone in the middle of the dance floor, laughing, him bending her backward, tango style, their arms creating a diamond of air. Why in front of all those people?

The remembering burns my face.



The girls, in the backseat of the car are busy coloring paper placemats from the Waffle House, their bellies full of pancakes, strawberries, and whipped cream,

Leo starts singing "Row, row, row your boat" and the girls join in. His singing is better than his dancing. The girls' voices are sweet as bells. The three of them keep the round going until Rag says, "Mom, sing." So I do. It's easier than not singing. And it doesn't take long before we're all silent again.

Both girls squeal when they spy the cows dotting the steep incline of the copper mine in Globe: cows in thick grass, cows plastered against the green hill, stuck like magnets on a bulletin board. The road winds up and down and over the railroad tracks. Weathered stone buildings give way to scattered fast-food restaurants.

After the turn-off, both highway and land flatten; the car hits 85. I tell Leo to slow down. Remind him about last year's speeding ticket. His answer is to press hard on the accelerator. The car jumps forward. I ask the girls if they have on their seatbelts, but forget to listen for answers.

Leo gobbles up miles. Jaw tight. Neck jutting forward. Leading with his nose. As if speeding will make the vacation go faster. Will get him back home to her. Rain hammers down, catching us in the mountains. Lightning tossed by Zeus. Thunder made by God's favorite bowling ball.

Over my shoulder, I see both girls have their seatbelts securely in place. Rag presses her nose against the window. Mop counts the wormy pelts of water against hers.

High grass, broken under the deluge, blurs by.

The storm disappears as quickly as it came. And like good pilgrims, we mark our progress. We've gone from Globe's "bulletin board" cows to the Dairy Queen in Show Low for Blizzards and hot dogs to the Pinetop Wal-Mart for suntan lotion, Kleenex, inhalers, cowboy boots for Rag.

The road ripples through goldenweed, penstemon, ponderosa, shimmering aspen. The sun touches a distant ridge. Then we're off the highway onto the dirt road.

It's been raining here too, and potholes, hidden by mud, rock and roll us. Leo doesn't slow down. Gravel spins up, pings against the undercarriage. The car bumps, clatters, fishtails. The girls titter nervously. I clutch the armrest. Brace my feet. Grit my teeth. We're nearing the T in the road where we turn right, but car slows only a little.

Across in a meadow near the pines, a deer raises her head. "Look!" I say, but —

27

The car brakes, spins, BAM.

My head bounces against the passenger door.

The girls screech, "Dad! Daddy! Daddeeee!"

Then we stop. Teeter on the crest of the ditch.

For a moment, we sit. Breathing hard. Sweating in spite of the air conditioner.

Leo puts the car in reverse. Gently presses the pedal. Eases us back onto the shoulder.

"What'd we hit?" I ask, remembering the deer, head up, at the edge of the forest.

"Stop sign." Leo takes off his seatbelt, pats my knee. "You okay?" Our eyes meet and I can see he's sorry. He reaches into the back seat. "You girls doing okay?"

Rag says, "Yeah," and sniffles.

Leo checks the damages. The stop sign looks like a demolished Tootsie Roll Pop, cherry-flavored. The car has a nasty gash in its hood.

Leo says, "It could've been worse."

"Yeah," I say. "We could be dead."


The road follows the creek – higher this year than usual – as it digs around hills thick with pine, cuts through rain-soaked meadows, wildflowers dappling the green. There's no denying the anticipation in the car as we curve around the final bend. Rock Mountain Ranch huddles in its deep valley, surrounded by national forest, sixty miles from the nearest interstate, seven thousand feet above the desert floor.

We greet the owners, an older couple, Gary and Reina Steward. Nice people, normal, uncomplicated, no kids. Gary, cowboy hat, plaid shirt, wrangler jeans, makes a joke about the dent in the front of the car. Leo laughs and shrugs, claims the Ford is his next art piece.

Chuckling, Gary slips his thumb into his belt loop. "Sorry to tell you, but no river ride last week, won't do one this week. Too hard to cross the Black."

Our cabin is on the other side of the creek. Usually a meandering trickle, it looks like a river tumbling through the pasture. No trestle for vehicles to cross, only a footbridge, so Leo plunges the car full-throttle into the racing water.

"Surfing the ranch! Yee-ha!" he shouts. The girls fall over each other laughing.

After dinner in the main house, we take turns in the shower and, exhausted, go to bed early. The girls' voices rise and fall in the room next to ours as they talk about the cabin's potbelly stove, count off the names of the new batch of kittens, the accident with the stop sign. Rag worries that we won't be able to get the car back over the creek to leave at the end of the week. Mop hopes we can't.

On our side of the wall, Leo clings to the edge of the bed, I cling to mine, as if between us we can balance our tiny raft on its churning surface and avoid the rocks below.

I ache to touch him. Even move my foot slightly in his direction, but he shifts away. Once again, memory gnaws at my heart. After hiding in the museum bathroom, I found Leo sitting at our table, making pyramid shapes out of napkins. I could have said, "Where's the girl?" I could've said, "You bastard." But I didn't. I sat down, Leo glancing up at me quickly, his face flushed. He said, "This works. See?" as he elevated one of the triangular napkins, turned it, and held it close to the other four. "The big one copper, two in bronze, one in silver, and this one gold. I like this negative space here." And he used his jaw to indicate the gap created by his positioning. That moment between Leo and the girl, recreated. Had I read more into it than what was there?

*

This morning, the damn birds chirp. Squirrels scrabble across the tin roof, a horse whinnies, and is answered by a chorus of equine greetings. I take a deep breath. I'm a thousand miles from that museum, but my thoughts are only seconds from that girl – and the empty space Leo created by lifting their arms.

Leo snores softly next to me, his dark unruly hair a bristle brush, his naked arm hard-muscled, copper-colored, his leg linked around mine. Spread out in the center of the bed, he seems to have abandoned his balancing act, letting sleep sweep him away.

My fingers hover just above his lips. We need to get over this. I need to get over this. I can forgive him. I will forgive him. And then I will be able to kiss his mouth again.


The pinto lets out a deep snort as she picks her way up Rock Mountain. I stroke her hot gleaming shoulder. "We're almost to the top."

Leo is ahead, talking to one of the wranglers, a kid of thirteen or so. I catch enough words to know they're debating the merits of basketball versus baseball. The kid is into LeBron James. Leo likes the symmetry of nine men and a diamond.

Twenty horses and twenty riders meander up these last few twists in the trail. The midmorning sun filters through leaves, glinting off the roaring creek. Water plunges over stones, rushes hard against its banks, floods the vegetation with the same steady persistence of Leo's Indy 500 race up the mountain.

I'll ask him again about the girl. Later this afternoon, we can hike to the ridge behind the cabin. This time I won't fling accusations at him. I won't go so crazy he instantly denies anything and everything. I'll give him a chance – the space – to tell me the truth.

The girls and I wait for lunch with the other guests on the mismatched sofas of the game room in the main house.

"Rag? Mop?" The woman in the Ralph Lauren gingham shirt smirks, looking around to make certain everyone in the lodge is paying attention. "Sounds like you girls belong in a bucket."

The girls chortle in unison. "The better to wipe up the floor with you!"

The woman gasps, then laughs, and everyone sitting around laughs too. Embarrassed, giggling, Rag and Mop race out, the screen door banging behind them.

I apologize to the woman. It was Leo who gave them the nicknames and Leo who gave them the comeback. I search the large room – all pine logs and braided rugs. My husband is nowhere in sight.

From the porch of our cabin, slightly elevated above the meadow and creek, I can see the corral where wranglers kick up dirt, shove each other playfully, and separate the foals from their mothers. I can hear the cries of the mares. The panicked bleats of their babies.

Rag and Mop race between the creek and the cabin, stacking up sticks on the grass, building a tiny town with a spectacular view of water and forest. They asked for tin foil in the kitchen, found horseshoes and nails at the corral, gathered rocks from hill behind the cabin. They are creative. Like their father.

31

Leo has taken the car. I don't know where he's gone. Fishing, he said. Or maybe he's racing down the mountain. To call that girl?

"Hey Mom!" Rag waves. The girls scamper through the damp grass, rosy with summer sun, arms and legs tan, feet bare, thick black hair tangled.

A cool breeze lifts my own dishwater hair. A cloud blots the sun. Raindrops spot the porch's steps. The smell of metal taints the wind.

How swollen the creek is. An unexpected current heaves beneath the surface. There must be a storm high up where the water begins.




When Leo comes back, he drives the car fast. Splashing into the high creek, plowing across, bumping up the bank. A chunk of black soil and spongy grass tumbles into the water. Mud gums the car's tires. A horizontal line, like the line on an old boat, divides the dusty top half of the car from the wetness of the creek.

He slams the car door. His face is grim. He carries ice. No fish.

"Daddy!" shouts Mop. "Come see our city."

"We used nails for lampposts. My idea," boasts Rag.

"In a while," says Leo.

The girls stand with the creek and pasture behind them, dirty hands, dirty knees, two pretty Gullivers creating their own Lilliput, watching as Leo and I disappear into the cabin.

I sit on the edge of the lumpy mattress, eyes focused on the linoleum floor. A fly pesters. Leo paces.

"Where did you go?" I ask, looking up at him.

He stands with his back to the window, his face shadowed. "You've done a good job with the girls," he says.

The shiny white scar along his forearm ripples slightly. Suddenly I want to strike it, but my hands are dead in my lap.

He folds his arms, his face is calm. This scares me more than flying 50 miles an hour up a wet country road.

"Gary's giving me a lift into Springerville. I'm going back to L.A. tonight."

Relief gushes into my belly. "You sold something. The parabola?"

"I'm leaving the marriage. Our marriage. If I go back tonight, I can move out while you're here. That'll make it easier for all of us."

My skin loosens as if a thread has been pulled. The frayed tatters that have held me together, give way. I slip from the bed to the floor, my spine jarred as it hits the linoleum. "What?"

"I don't want to be married anymore."

I gulp air. Stare at his feet. One of his Nikes is untied. The soles of his shoes, the shoestring, are all black with mud. "Don't – what?"

The curtain made from old sheets flaps around him, the rain outside assaulting the cabin's tin roof. "I'm sorry. What else can I say?"

"What about the girls?"

"I love the girls." He pushes himself away from the sill, holds out a hand to help me up, but I smack it away.

Rag's laughter peals out. A squirrel cheeters in a nearby pine.

I mutter, "I knew it. I knew it when I saw you two together, but I couldn't, couldn't believe –"

"Melina isn't the issue."

"Melina?"

Then, suddenly, a shriek. Is it me, letting out some demon inside me or –

Someone's yelling. Rag.

What does she want?

But her voice, her screams, cut through me. I'm up.

Leo's out the door and down the steps. Toward the creek. Muck and sticks flying as he clomps through the girls' tiny city. Rain pelts my face. Where are they?

He's running along the wet bank, his feet slipping and sliding.

I pound after him. And see Rag stumbling ahead of him waving her hands, reaching toward the water, shouting, reaching—

NO.

They're both in the water.

"Regina! Mar—" I slip on slick weeds, forearms whacking dirt. Scramble up. Crying now. Wiping hair from eyes. Staring at the turbulent creek until I spy Mop. She's swimming, isn't she? She can swim. But she's thrashing. And Rag's in the water too, and the water is swelling, swallowing them around a curve. Leo dives in, head first.

I come up fast to the slippery bank. Mud and grass crumble, giving way and I tumble into the creek. Ice. My foot skids on a rock and I go down. Under, gulping. Scramble up. Cough. Struggle to catch my breath.

Rain hammers down. Shouts. Screams. People racing along the creek. Past where I can see.

I fight to climb back up the bank. Dig at the mud with my fingers. Water swats my side. Someone grasps my hands and pulls me out.

Dizzy. Water clogging my throat, I still manage to roar, "My girls!"


Rain splashes on a dome of steel and glass, the sky is broken into pieces, bruised black and blue. The smell of fuel. What is this place?

Through the open door, drizzle between us, stands Leo, his face to the ground. I remember how he bent her back, shaping an arc, a triangle, a diamond. Silver and gold in the dim gallery light.

"You okay?" A stranger's voice. I flinch.

"What?" In a slow glutinous motion, I tear my eyes from Leo toward the sound.

The stranger's lumpy, indistinct. Sadness seems to shroud his face. "We're ready to leave," he says, and in the darkness, I catch a glint of iris. I glance around. Glass and steel, not silver. My mind begins to click into place. I'm in a helicopter. The man in the seat is the pilot.

Leo's ashen face floats outside in the rain. And beyond him stands a crowd in slickers, mumbling. I glance down at my wet jeans. Mud.

Rushing water. The creek. Leo running.

"Ma'am? We're ready to leave."

There's another man, some kind of medic, in the copter with me. Crouched on the floor. He says, "Change your mind, Ma'am?"

I turn toward Leo, force steel into my voice, my eyes. "No. He can't come."

The medic, young, tan, maybe some Apache in him, exchanges a look with the pilot. The pilot shrugs, turns around in his seat.

Outside, Gary, holding onto his dripping hat, moves next to Leo.

The ground beneath me begins to tilt. Then we lift, wobbling, into the air. Circle the creek. Angle into the purple sky.

I turn toward the floor where my daughters lay wrapped at my feet. I touch Regina's cold forehead. Margaret's white cheek.

The rain turns to hail.

# Landscape

She wakes in the shadows of their bedroom, slipping out at five so she can run to Montana Avenue and back by the time her husband ties his tie and rumbles downstairs for coffee. She brews French Roast before she leaves and he's drinking it when she returns smelling of morning and sweat, the house filled with the aroma of freshly ground beans. She pecks his cheek and makes his oatmeal.

A day comes when, without really thinking about it, she turns left at the corner of Montana instead of right. She jogs under shady oaks past unfamiliar fences, lush lawns, glancing down the road ahead where clusters of purple irises poke through a bed of rocks. She isn't lost, she's exploring, and the air hints of spring. Her lips curl into a smile. She gets back later than usual, her husband waiting for breakfast. When she slices the banana, she slices her thumb, a sharp little pain, specks of blood landing in the cornflakes. Milk washes them away.

She runs by the irises every day until they die and only rocks remain. The ground is freshly turned, peat moss added. The small boulders remind her of hot summer hikes when she was a teenager. One time she wore the wrong kind of shoes, flip-flops not optimal on stony surfaces, and she'd turned her ankle. Not broken, not sprained, but strained.

She plops on the curb with her back to the rocks and puts her head between her knees, ignoring the drone of suburban traffic, and remembers the mountain, the meadow, the sky so bright, the sweet grass of long ago.

When she arrives home, her husband's gone, his coffee cup ignored, his breakfast bowl untouched in the cupboard.

# Losing Ground

It began with hands. Doesn't it always? Fingers lightly brushing wrists. Thumbs in palms. Remove the bracelet. Remove the watch. Clothes go next. Stinky fish hands touching here. Touching there.

The memory splits her in two. Then drives her down the rough wooden stairs to the dock.

Claudine's no sentimentalist, her. Not after years of working in the sheriff's office, answering phones, filing paperwork, watching folks in handcuffs pass her desk, giving her the look. But now, even with that, she's breaking apart inside.

She climbs into the pirogue and uses the pole to push away from the soft bank. Light tints the eastern sky. A breeze comes in from the gulf to fill her nose with salt. The camp, high on stilts, soon disappears behind a stand of salt-soaked cypress. She closes her eyes, lets the boat drift.

She's buried herself down the bayou since Madge died, parking her little Dodge under the house next to her brother's fishing boat. She's asked her family to stay away. At least for a while. If she remained in town, anybody might drop by without so much as a knock on the front door. She needs to be alone in the swamp, with its rich brackish smell and slow mossy currents.

Claudine lets the water push her toward the sea. Remembers that first summer she asked Madge to the camp. Madge was married then, her kids just babies, but she left them in Houma for a "girls weekend." They played cards and made gumbo. They drank and went fishing.

Madge, a deputy who took Claudine under her wing when she started work at the sheriff's, said she was too soft. Told her, "The world is full of assholes, and the sooner you accept that, the better off you'll be." Strong friends they became, two women weathering hurricanes and money troubles, Claudine steady through Madge's divorce, Madge a rock when Claudine lost a brother to a drunk driver. Still, it took ten years to begin.

They were down the bayou, cutting mullet for bait. They were laughing, mugs of French coffee steaming on the slats of the dock, their fingers reaching in the bucket, the sky just beginning to streak gray. Claudine's hand accidently bumped Madge's, and Madge took it, and kissed her wrist, her palm, the hollow at the center.

Now Madge is gone, shot in the neck by a stray bullet during the takedown of a bank robber.

Claudine stands up to pole the boat, the wind chilling her wet cheeks.

The gulf itself isn't as far as it used to be, not since Katrina brought salt water pouring into fresh. Burying land, trees, houses, killing wildlife. Claudine thinks about the vastness of water beyond the continental shelf, its cold beckoning expanse. She sits down again, sets aside the pole, and begins to row toward the fading horizon.

# Wounded Moon

M ason took a slice of Spam onto the cabin steps so he could bay at the moon. Sometimes he thought he heard wolves answering from the pines, or maybe just coyotes. His plaid pajamas were stiff from sweat and the evaporated milk he'd spilled a couple of days before. The flannel gave off a pungent smell, a strategic weapon against the incursion of pests, both the four- and two-legged kind.

He wiped his fingers on the step and belched a meaty burp. Rummaged in his pocket for his last blunt. Felt the weight of his lighter instead. He pulled it out and held it between his thumb and forefinger. Amanda had given it to him, his initials engraved in Edwardian script. He was surprised he had it on him. He used to keep it polished, but now in the strong moonlight, he saw dark whorls of tarnish on the metal. He started to toss it into the high grass, but caught himself, and dropped it back in his pocket. He studied the sky. Emptied his head.

These summits between Mason and the moon were one-sided, the man in the night sky being taciturn by nature, but then, nobody talked to Mason any more. Nobody except for the kid. And the kid was not one to chat.

Three months after he'd arrived at the cabin, with its galvanized pump over a primitive sink and an outhouse under the firs, Mason began to notice how night after night the moon constantly changed. Slowly, but persistently. Waning moon, new, waxing crescent, first quarter, turning gibbous, full. It was full now, a deep yellowish-red, all the ridges and valleys visible. What month was it? September? October? A hunter's moon. A blood moon.

During the day Mason jotted down his lunar observations, doodling in the margins, his pen absently tracing craters and darkening seas within lop-sided circles. Writing had been Dr. Leggett's idea, a journal of thoughts, daily affirmations, the subject matter irrelevant. So Mason wrote, getting down everything he knew about the moon. He liked where it led him. The pages of text ate the hours. The almost-poems shimmered in slanted light through the small cabin window, and his drawings, too, the yellow cuticle against an inked-in sky, the plump roundness of the moon in full.

Eventually, he asked the kid to buy him a book, something along the lines of *The Idiot's Guide to the Moon*. All this interest in lunar activities seemed like a good sign to Mason, although he never let the word "recovery" take permanent residence in his mind.

Could he trust the kid to get him more weed? Maybe. But it didn't matter. He'd have the bourbon. He settled against the porch post, shivering as a breeze slipped under his smelly flannel pajama top. Did anything matter? Nope.

Mason asked the kid to bring him tubes of tennis balls with his next weekly order of Spam, potato chips, evaporated milk, and alcohol.

"Yellow," he said. Eight fuzzy yellow orbs. He'd found the string, dug out from the bottom of the old hunter's toolbox behind the potbelly stove. And there were plenty of sticks in the yard.

"You'll owe me gas money," the kid said as he dumped the grocery bags onto the pine table, a bottle of Makers' thumping out. "Wal-Mart's not around the fucking corner."

41

Mason rubbed his wiry beard, then his hair, both getting out-of-hand. He shrugged, wondered again about the weed. He considered the kid's Jimi Hendrix sweatshirt, his baggy cargo shorts, giant sneakers. They weren't so far apart in age. Maybe under different circumstances they might've been friends. Well, not friends exactly. More like brothers.

"So what'd ya need tennis balls for anyway?" asked the kid.

"I'll show you next time."

"Can't. This is my last trip."

A tiny jolt shot through the back of Mason's neck. "Why?"

"Starting college."

"You don't want to do that. It's bullshit."

"Yeah, well, irregardless, I'm going. You owe me $87.52 plus tip."

Mason broke the seal on the bourbon, took a sip, and got his checkbook from a drawer by the sink.


The single bed was shoved in the corner of the cabin where the front windows faced east, the sun sending its daily glow over his creased face, rousing him. This moment each day, like the moment he'd tossed his Prozac down the glory hole in the outhouse, made him almost feel alive again. Almost.

Then he heard the stuttering diesel engine of an ancient Mercedes-Benz. His hangover kicked in.

Shit.


"Mason! Wake up." His mother peered in through the window. Rapped on the glass.

"I'm up," he said, sniffing under his arm as he opened the door. "What're you doing here?"

She pecked him on the cheek, rubbed her hands together. "Get that fire going, will you?"

Mason walked to the iron stove in the corner. The lever felt warm even though the fire from the night before had long since died. "What's happened? Dad okay?"

He took an old *LA Times* from a pile on the floor and crammed torn pieces into the stove, added a few twigs. From the table he grabbed a box of matches, dug inside for a red-tipped stick and, striking it, edged the flame along the newspaper. He blew into the iron belly and piece by piece inserted uneven chunks of wood.

Warmth quickly filled the tiny space and they stood there, quite close, without talking, the room turning amber with sunlight.

His mother held her hands together, no longer kneading them. Her blue eyes were blank, her mouth neutral. All the anxiety she'd shown when she came in, the insistence at the door and window, had vanished.

Mason shifted away first. "Coffee?" he asked, retreating to the sink. He shook the full kettle, and clanked it onto the cast iron stove. His mother sat down at the table, picked up and read one of the sheets of yellow-lined paper scattered there.

"That boy called me. He can't bring you supplies anymore," she said.

"I'll find someone else."

"You'll find? *You'll* find! You don't find anything anymore. You don't *do* anything. I'm the one who has to take care of it."

"I'm sorry," he said, not even thinking about the words.

Her mouth fretted at the corner. She was a stranger to him, this old woman with gray at the roots of her dyed hair, lines around her mouth, a new thinness in her shoulders.

"I've had enough." She waved the sheet of paper at him, let it float to the cracked linoleum floor. "This hermit thing, this whole living-in-the-forest-like-Thoreau shit. Look at you. You're a mess. You stink. Why are you torturing me like this?"

"I'm not trying to torture anyone, least of all you." He retrieved the paper – it was the blueprint for his cycles-of-the-moon model – and sat softly onto the other chair. "I'm trying to stop torturing myself."

"For God's sake, Mason, it wasn't your fault." She leaned in, her jaw set. He could feel her breath on his face, smell the slight sourness of early morning. "Your Amanda is getting married, you hear me? You were building a life and now you're letting it slip away."

Mason pulled back, his mother moving into the space he vacated. "She's concerned about you. Doesn't want to hurt you. She asked me to tell you how sorry she is." She paused, leaned even closer. "She wants you to stop her."

"She's getting on with her life. That's good. Good for her." The words coming from his throat were choked with fog and distance. Still he met her gaze.

"Not good for her, Mason. Don't you want her back? Don't you want anything back?"

Dust motes danced in an angle of light. A jay called outside the window. Several taunted in response. The kettle squealed. Mason scraped his chair back along the bare wood floor.

"If you won't come back for Amanda, come back for me," she said.

He brought the kettle over and focused on pouring hot water into cups, stirring in Nescafé and powdered creamer, setting the plastic mug in front of her. "I'm not coming home."

She scowled. Neither of them said a word until she got up and put her jacket on. "This is killing your father."

She strode to the cabin door and opened it. Before she went through, she faced him.

"I don't feel sorry for you, Mason. You feel sorry enough for the both of us." Then she was gone, the door gaping open.

He followed her. Leaned against the jamb, watched the old Mercedes crunch over gravel until the forest swallowed it up.

Yay for Amanda. She hadn't stood by him, and Mason didn't blame her. He was sure the man she picked would believe in the same things he himself had once believed in, the value of a big San Francisco law firm, golf on weekends, and sterling silver lighters.

He let his body slide down the doorframe, landing hard on the threshold. He felt a splinter in his palm and pressed it deeper, but the pain wasn't enough.

The images blazed. Him speeding down the 101, distracted and tired, cool air rushing in through the open window, a fingernail moon hanging over the ocean. His cell phone burped. He took it from the cup holder, Amanda texting: "I'm waiting. Hrrrry," him laughing, texting back, "Hrrrrying." A horn. A car that shouldn't have been there. A girl's face in the passenger window, black-rimmed glasses flying.

Not his fault according to the witness who saw the other car cut in front of him. But he knew. He knew.

Staggering to his feet, he shook his head hard, harder, then banged it against the cabin doorframe. Swung around and whacked it against a porch post. Not once, not twice, but three times, until he tumbled down the rough wooden steps into the dirt, rolling until he stopped, bloodied face up. He screwed his eyes shut as the sun tipped over the cabin's tin roof, and willed himself not to breathe, but his lungs made him suck in the acrid scent of burning wood from the chimney, the smell of decomposing pine.

He stayed in the dirt the rest of the day and into the night, unable to move, not wanting to move, certain he was concussed, hoping he was, drifting in and out of sleep and delirium. When he woke just before dawn, the moon lay low in the black sky, bandaged in cloud. The chill penetrated his pajamas, nipped his toes. He labored to his feet, head throbbing, and trudged up the porch steps.

Inside the dark cabin, he bumped into the table, his hand banging against something, a splash of wetness shocking him. The smell of stale coffee.

Amanda's face, his mother's pinched mouth, the flight of black-rimmed glasses crowded his thoughts as the morning bleached the room until the pump over the sink became real, the bed in the corner, the table in front of him, the spill of coffee.

He snapped up a crumpled piece of paper and swiped at the brown streaks. Grabbed another sheet and swiped again, and another, and another, the liquid, creeping in watery vines along the wood until Mason found himself turning from the table and shoving every sheet of paper – his writing, his doodles, his plan for the phases-of-the-moon model, all of it – into the maw of the cast iron stove. Then, pulling the tarnished silver lighter from his pajama pocket, he set the tinder aflame.

# Tools of the Trade

Sharp things. Needles. Knives. My father's rusty hacksaw. I love them all. People surrender secrets when I flash a meat thermometer and remind them of what it feels like to be a Thanksgiving turkey. Would you like me to take your temperature? My safe deposit box is crammed with loot courtesy of my mother's paring knife. It's not just for peeling anymore. Several little slits along someone's belly work like several little mouths. But the hacksaw performs the best. That row of jagged teeth knows how to persuade. And the rust. Everyone fears the rust.

# Heaven Spoils

Black clouds dome the sky, the color blue forgotten. Rain drowns tomatoes and strips the fig tree outside my window. It's kept on for weeks, those fat drops hammering the roof. Inside, Mother reads about Noah. She watches for arks.

Father dies, then Danny dies. Maybe the pox, we don't know for sure. No neighbors on our lonely road. No doctor for a hundred miles. Water and sludge make digging graves impossible. We wrap them both in potato sacks, and drag them through the storm and into the shed; whisper prayers, lock the door.

The house has become a dank basement. Water seeps through every seam, warps wood, turns flour to paste. The cold is everywhere, in the bed sheets, in my underwear. Clothes cling to skin. Hair clings to scalp. We burn the kitchen chairs for warmth.

Mother sends me to the chicken coop. The mud in the yard – deep and heavy and thick – sucks off my shoes, so I fall to my knees and crawl. Inside, where the stench is wrenching, I find no eggs and one quivering hen in the corner.

After the bird is eaten, the candles burned, I tell my mother we have to go. She doesn't look up from her psalms. I pack our things. Help her with her oilskin slicker.

We take the Bible, some tattered dollar bills, the remaining cans of tuna and beans and the last of our water, a tent, and two umbrellas. Mother grips my arm as we slog along. I wish I could read the mud the same way people from the north can read the snow.

The umbrellas snap and the tent begins to tear. Mother dies on the fifth night. I curse her for taking the easy way out and kick around in the sludge, pulling my hair. Then I curse myself, dropping to the soggy ground and beg for her forgiveness. I curl beside her, head tucked into her shoulder, rain pelting down like dirt on a grave.

A dream creeps in. Mother is in the kitchen with a wooden mallet in her hand, tenderizing the shanks of our cow. Sun slants through the kitchen window. Outside, birds peck at figs. Father tills the field and Danny, in the chicken coop, fixes wire. I am not there.

When I wake, I wipe the muck from Mother's face and crossing her arms, tuck the Bible underneath, cover her with branches from dying trees, and trudge on.

Along the invisible road ahead, rain drums down. Mud disappears under rising water. My shoes are paper, my toes and fingers numb. Raindrops burn my eyes.

I listen for the whine of planes; watch for car lights flashing in the distance. I am all that is left of those I know. I keep an eye out for any kind of ark.

# Oranges

She's small, waif-like, this girl/woman who stands by the freeway onramp with her American flag vest and her bags of oranges. Black stockings below that vest. Legs like straws. No. Legs like those sticks they use to stir coffee.

Cars whiz past her outstretched hand, rushing to catch the yellow traffic light, leaving me with a red. I lean out the window of my Jetta and offer her my uneaten scone. She doesn't smile, a small hoop through her bottom lip, her words mumbled. "Oranges. Cheap. They're good."

"No thanks," I say, and extend my arm, shaking the napkin-wrapped pastry. "For you. I haven't taken a bite."

She backs toward the black-and-white left-turn arrow planted in cement and glares at me. An impatient horn bleats, the light now green, so I shrug and head down the onramp and into the stream of commuter traffic.

Somewhere between Glendale and Burbank, the oranges girl steals into my head, her big eyes, huge charcoal smudges like those kids in the prints my grandmother used to have in her bedroom, no older than fourteen or fifteen. Then I'm exiting the freeway at Olive and heading for my office where I write food copy: Tangy and Delicious. 100% Fat Free! Like oranges.

I slip my key card into the slot for employee parking, the yellow and black arm lifts, thin like her body, and decide I will buy oranges from the girl on the onramp – no matter how much citric acid blisters my mouth.

Women who get divorced at forty and have no children usually adopt cats. I have goldfish instead – less maintenance that way – orange fantails named Flip and Flop, in a twenty-gallon tank. They swim to the top when I come through the door after work and tap on their glass, dust their water with flakes. Individuals both, better than cats. Tonight, while I eat my lamb chop, I watch them circle the tiny castle at the bottom of their aquarium and wonder how many oranges that girl on the onramp has to eat before her lips begin to pucker.

The bags are $3.00 per, so the next day I give the girl five bucks. She hands me the oranges and hunts for change. When I wave her off, she frowns. I toss the heavy bag onto the passenger seat. My car smells like Jamba Juice.

Beyond my little balcony, the sun deepens to coral. I sit at my table and eat a bagel with melted cheese for dinner. Sip some wine. Watch my fish. They're chubby with bubble lips, yet smoothly graceful. I wonder how Flip would feel about a lip ring. If I had a daughter, would we fight over piercings?

The following day, I buy more oranges. Six bucks for two netted bags, no discount. She takes my money and tromps off to peddle her wares to the people behind me, not even a thank-you. Well, I think, that's it for me. Still I watch her in my rear view mirror and notice the hole in her stocking.


Once home, I throw the sacks onto the kitchen counter. Now I have a couple of dozen oranges. I turn on *Jeopardy*. Alex's voice follows me through the condo, quizzing me with answers. I ask, "Who is Britney Spears?" from the toilet. "What is *Oliver?*" from the kitchen. I pluck an orange off the counter, rip the peel. Eat. Juice runs down my chin. The taste is slightly bitter. Later in bed my tongue worries the sore spots.


Sunday afternoon I visit my mother at her three-stage living facility – independent, assisted, total care. She's in assisted now that she's fallen twice and broken her arm and wrist. I bring *US* magazine and oranges. She wants to talk Angelina Jolie and the selfishness of adopting foreign-born kids when so many American babies have no place to live. I'd rather talk about how Brad Pitt deserted Jennifer Aniston the same day Ian left me. I help my mother work out who at the home deserves her wealth of fruit. She orders me to bring more.

I dream Brad Pitt leaves Angelina for me and we adopt the oranges girl or we try to adopt her, but then Brad goes and sleeps with her or Britney Spears, or maybe both. I can't remember.


On Monday, the girl isn't at her spot. The twenty-dollar bill I've brought to buy more oranges stays curled in my cup holder. I fret that she's sick or thrown into juvie.

*

Later at work, I find myself pondering milk cartons and wondering why they don't put pictures of lost kids on them anymore. Who is out there to report the onramp oranges girl missing? Only me?

My condo's 1400 square feet with a large alcove and closet off the entry. The alcove is stacked with boxes. If I get rid of them, there'd be room for a futon. My mother calls to tell me everyone at the retirement home wants See's candy instead of fruit. I feed the fish and turn on *Jeopardy*. Ask the TV, "What is a sin of omission?"

On Tuesday, the girl is back. I watch as she lifts a bag of oranges into the cab of the truck ahead of me. The signal changes from red to green, and the guy in the truck takes off without paying. Asshole. I could make the light, but I stop instead. Horns blare. The twenty-dollar bill is still in its nest from yesterday. I offer it to the girl. She snatches the money and starts to shove sacks of oranges at me, one after another.

"No. No," I say. "I'm paying for the truck driver."

Those dark eyes penetrate mine, her skinny arms relentless until the bags crash to the pavement, break open, oranges rolling and bouncing into the street. A horn shrieks behind me, the light goes yellow, and I hit the accelerator, plump citrus grinding and smashing under the tires and then I'm yelling "Sorry! Sorry!" as I descend onto the freeway.

# Something About L.A.

He puts me out of the Beamer south of Four Corners, pissed because they've closed the monument for construction. Not my fault but he has to blame someone.

A hot wind smacks my face as he takes off across the high desert, leaving me in motor exhaust and sand. He wouldn't even let me have my Gucci purse, my Louis V. suitcase, or my handle of vodka. Now I'm worried about my sandals, Jimmy Choos, the sun already burning stripes across my insteps.

I spy willows in the distance. If I find water, maybe I'll be okay. It's not like I was born to money anyway. Not me.

I don't get a half a mile before I hear a clatter from somewhere behind me, bumping and bouncing over rock and sand and scrub. An old pickup truck, rust eating its way across the hood, catches up to me.

At first I feel relief, but when I can't see anyone in the front seat, my heart jolts, me wondering if this is one of those Stephen King moments when the surreal bumps into some poor sucker's reality. I don't believe in ghost El Caminos, but my eyes aren't deceiving me.

The truck shivers to a stop, dust swirling. The door opens as a small figure slides off the driver's seat. A boy, just a boy, dark skin and hair, wearing a faded plaid shirt and jeans. Barefoot.

Puts his hands on hips and says, "I ain't gonna hurt you."

"I guess not." I'm feeling better now knowing I've got 50 pounds on him. "What are you, ten?"

"Twelve. You lost?" he asks.

"My boyfriend kicked me out of the car. He's probably in Utah by now."

"What'd you do?"

"I didn't do anything. He got mad because they've got that Four Corners place all torn up. They wouldn't let him sprawl across all four states at once."

"Seems like a lot of you people think that's important."

"Not me. I'm heading to L.A."

"You famous?"

I smile at this because, of course, that's why I'm going to L.A. Best place to get your face on the cover of the *Enquirer*. I look him up and down. "You're a good driver. Not just anyone could make it across rocky ground."

"I do okay."

"You wanna give me a ride to Farmington?"

"No way, but I won't let you die out here. Name's Ruben."

"Kim."

We rattle into Shiprock, Ruben telling me we're on the "Rez." He's Navajo, everyone's Navajo. Then I spot Gilbert's car. Holler, "Stop the truck!"

Ruben, cool as he seems, isn't immune to a woman's screams and slams the brake. I stumble out before the El Camino comes to a stop and race over to the dusty BMW in front of a diner. Peer in the driver's side window. Yep, there's my Gucci bag. I yank on the door handle, but it's locked. Smack my palm on the glass and shout, "Gilbert!"

I'm hot and sweaty and angrier than I've ever been. "Gilllllll-BERT!"

I head for the diner. The cold blast from an overactive air conditioner takes the breath right out of my chest. Gilbert, in his Tommy Bahama shirt, swivels away from the counter to smile at me. He looks so calm I feel as if I've misunderstood what's happened to me. Of course I haven't.

He says, "You ready to apologize?"

"I could've died out there."

"Looks like you didn't. You might need a shower though."

"That's what you say after dumping me?"

Gilbert slaps a twenty onto the counter and slips off his stool. Strolls over and grips my upper arm. "You'll feel better once we're on the road."

"Let me go." I set my feet, stiffen my body, resist.

He drags me toward the door, but boy Ruben puts himself between Gil and the exit. He may be twelve, but he's got a man's confidence. Everyone in the diner is watching, and it takes me a second to realize part of Ruben's confidence comes from knowing all the customers, halfway through their cheeseburgers and fries, have his back. So this is what community – loyalty – looks like.

Gilbert, squeezing my arm, weighs his chances. Though he doesn't give a shit about me, he'd rather die than let me go, but outnumbered, he does. My arm stings.

Still, Ruben won't let him out. He stands there facing down Gilbert who looms above him.

"She needs her stuff," says Ruben. "All of it."

Gilbert's face goes red as chili peppers, but the diners, even the cook from behind the counter, crowd around us. Gilbert glares at me. "Bitch."

Outside again, the air is broiling. Beads of sweat the size of dimes pop along Gilbert's forehead. The BMW chirps twice and the trunk pops open. One of the lunch crowd reaches in and removes my Louis V. suitcase and my vodka while another swings open the front passenger door and takes my purse.

Gilbert jumps in his car, swearing about "this god-forsaken hell hole," adding a few choice words for me, until he finally roars away with the lid of the trunk flapping behind him. Everyone laughs and pats Ruben on the shoulder. Suddenly I feel lost, seeing what it's like to belong.

The men filter back into the diner, leaving my alcohol and purse on the suitcase. Ruben strolls over.

"Guess I gotta thank you," I say.

"Might be nice since I saved your ass."

"You did, didn't you? Thank you. You're mama must be proud."

The boy shrugs, looks at the ground, kicks dust with his big toe.

"Well," I say. "I owe you one."

Ruben turns toward his truck. I watch, biting my lip, wondering where I'm going to find a bus way out here.

He opens the passenger side door and bows. "Get in."

"Thought you wouldn't take me to Farmington."

"That's right. I won't." Then he ticks through his fingers. "I can sing, I can dance, and someone's gotta watch your back – so guess what? We're going to L.A."

"I don't think you can do that."

"Sure I can. There's my uncle." He points to the man, dressed like a cook, hovering in the doorway of the diner, letting out all the cold air. "Ask him."

I shout, "Is it okay? Really?"

The uncle ambles over, pulling his hands from inside his apron to load my suitcase and vodka into the back of the truck. "School starts in a couple weeks. If he's not in a movie by then, send him on back."

Ruben, grinning behind the wheel, fires up the engine. I climb in, his uncle handing me my Gucci purse, shutting the door behind me, and pressing down on the lock.

"I'll take good care of him," I say.

"He'll take care of *you*."

I laugh and sit back against the truck's worn upholstery, buoyant as Ruben hangs a U-ie and heads west.

57

# Starkville

I wait tables at the Starkville Diner out on Desert Highway, about a mile before the first real intersection in town. Donnie lets me wear jeans and t-shirts, thank goodness, instead of one of those gold-colored uniforms with the scratchy white collars and starched aprons my mom wore back when she, as she likes to put it, "slung hash."

Donnie runs a Spartan little place here, easy for two people to handle, no real kitchen, the grill a one-eighty behind me. But I'm alone tonight because it's the boss's anniversary. Forty-three years with the same person. Not many marriages like that these days.

The place is empty so I've got time to ponder on what I'm going to do with my daughter. She's barely twelve and already has breasts. They say it's the hormones they pump into chickens that does it. And from what I remember about ages thirteen-fourteen – living in a small town – I don't want that for Beth. It's time to get out, head somewhere that has a winter to it, where blue geese dip through gray skies and old men build wooden houses on icy lakes. Someplace, not too small, not too big. Suburbia, with real snow.

I'm wiping down the counter for the millionth time when the door opens letting in the sharp smell of sage and a white-haired old guy, head down, wearing a plaid jacket and polyester pants. His legs seem so thin and crooked they could be made of Manzanita.

He takes me by surprise. I slip my half-filled Pepsi glass off the counter.

"Hey," he says. "You got pie?"

"Lemon meringue, no berry." I straighten up, tossing the rag into the tub next to my glass, and before I can stop myself, I'm smoothing down my hair with a damp hand. There's something about this guy. Like I should know him, but I don't.

"Lemon'll do." He slides onto the stool opposite me. Puts his bony, spotted hands on the Formica. I let my eyes flick to his worn face and away. A down-on-his-heels geezer. They're passing through most days now, more and more.

"Coffee?"

"Don't drink the stuff. You got whiskey?"

This makes me stiffen. An alkie. I pull the lever on the hot water. Grab a basket of tea bags and place it in front of him. "How 'bout some herb tea?"

He digs through the assortment, holds up a scarlet packet. "Only if you got Red Zinger."

Nodding, I watch as he wrestles with the wrapper. I glance outside into the dark, then say, "Didn't hear a car. Someone drop you off?"

"Yep. Hitched from California."

"Aren't you going the wrong direction? Most people are heading toward California."

"Been there, done that. Got my pie?"

I slide the spatula under soggy crust, try to shake off a tremor of unease. When I put the slice in front of him, he's staring at me.

He says, "You really don't know who I am, do you?"

I get a little dizzy as the words line up as a sentence in my head. Do I know who he is?

He takes a forkful of pie. "Kelly, think about it."

"How do you know my name?" I feel for my badge. Not there. Squint at his faded green eyes, crooked front tooth.

59

The same, but not the same. My head goes fizzy. I step back, hit my arm against the hot coffee urn. Yelp. Pain judders through me.

The man – Ray – leaps up, dish and fork clattering to the linoleum, and scoots around the counter. "What the hell? Are you nuts?"

He pushes me toward the ice-maker near the sink. Filling the counter cloth with crushed ice, he places it gently against the burn. Holds it there. We're standing close to each other now, and I begin to tremble. Ray Clary here, in this diner, an old man now with white hair and wrinkles mapping his suddenly familiar face.

"What – what happened to you?" I stammer. But I know. Booze, drugs. He was skidding when he left, a drinker in a drinking town.

Finally he says in a low and weary voice, "I've been a stupid man."

An eighteen-wheeler crunches the gravel outside, brakes spitting. Ray, because it *is* Ray, drops the dishrag into the tub. Melted ice courses down my arm as we hear the truck door slam, a grunt and yawn, the scrape of feet. It feels like one of those slo-mo movie moments. Finally I whisper, "I – I have to work," and Ray slips from behind the counter just as a heavyset driver strides in.

I ask the trucker to flip the open sign around to "CLOSED." Serve him coffee, slap a hamburger on the grill, and keep an eye on Ray, now slouched in the booth by the restrooms.

I can see the younger Ray in him, the one I used to know. The slight angle of his head, the fans of wrinkles around his gray eyes, and of course, his hands laid out in front of him side by side on the table. I should've seen it right away. But how could I? He was more than ten years older than me, and now looks twenty, even thirty years more. And I wasn't expecting him, couldn't expect him, not now, not ever, really. He swore he'd never come back and in

60

that moment of remembering, a forgotten longing slips through me, the smell of his sweat, his hand on my belly, his lips on my nipples.

My daughter Beth darts into my head. She's at my mom's right now like she always is when I'm at work, the two of them playing Double Solitaire at the dining table, Beth's swinging legs visible through its glass top, Mom's cigarettes fogging the light fixture.

"Miss?" The truck driver's voice brings me back. He's pointing to the sizzling burger under my spatula. I flip it, hunt for cheese and a zip-lock of lettuce, onion, and tomato in the fridge. Pouring a mug of coffee, I set it and the last slice of lemon meringue in front of my customer, saying, "Dessert's on me," then turn to plate his burger and fries and serve them next to the pie. He gives me a big grin and digs in.

I glance at Ray who is taking it all in. This time I don't feel any longing for this man who used to fill all the space around me with breathless heat. What runs through me now is – what? Sorrow, regret, shame?

Shame for sure, because back then, my mom made sure of it, throwing my suitcase out the front door where it split open and my black bra lay spidered on the sidewalk for all the neighborhood to see. And they were there, Steve the Sleaze working on his Harley in his wife-beater t-shirt and filthy cargo shorts, Nancy Thompson from next door hosing down her scraggly oleanders. Even Mr. Gettich, the retired math teacher from the high school, stood out on his lawn, his morning *Gazette* clutched in one hand, a stogy in the other.

The sun was blazing. It must've been noon and Mom was yelling. I thought the vein in her forehead was gonna pop.

I stomped out of the house, stepped over the suitcase, climbed into my old Honda, and took off.

That first night in Reno, Ray played Twenty-one and won $2700. He bought me a tight red dress and a pair of diamond studs. They were small but they were real.

We drank until we could barely stumble into the honeymoon suite. We made sloppy love just inside the door. I know because I woke up curled under the little table in the entry, the bed still virgin, Ray gone back out to the casino.

He lost what was left of the money he'd won. I should've known then we were in trouble. Six months later we had Beth and I didn't see my mother for six years.


"Excuse me, Miss?" Again it's the truck driver pulling me out of deep thought. "A little more coffee?"

"Oh, sorry. I don't know what's gotten into me. How's the pie?" I grab the metal pot and slosh it into his mug.

The trucker inclines his chin toward Ray, says, "That guy bothering you because —"

"It's okay. I know him." I'm whispering, not sure why.

His thick eyebrows shove together as he shifts on the stool to give Ray a hard look. "I can take care of him."

"No thanks. I'm fine." I shake my head, write up a ticket, and slip it under his coffee mug.

After the semi pulls out of the lot, Ray comes over and takes the plate off the counter, walks it around, and puts it into the sink. Turns on the water.

I grab a dishrag and head to the door, lock it, and start wiping down the four-tops. Trying to scour away the tension of the last twenty minutes. Worried about the next twenty.

Ray says, "You still got your admirers, I see."

I shove chairs into place, move to the booth, and swipe across the table. Then I whip toward him. "Why are you here? Just tell me in case I have to go home and get my shotgun and shoot you."

"Hold on." He holds up soapy hands. "I'm not going to mess up your life. I promise."

"Well, that just isn't possible, is it? Not unless you go on back to California this minute."

"I didn't come to make things hard for you."

"Then why the hell are you here?"

He turns his back, continues with the dishes, says, "I don't have any place else to go."

"Great! Just great." I throw the towel down. Look around for something else to throw. "You want Beth, don't you? You're going to try and take her away from me. Well, she doesn't need you."

I'm shaking so hard, it's like I'm not going to be able to keep my feet. My nose is running, my eyes wet.

Ray turns around. Says with a soft slur in his voice, "Sit down, Kelly, before you fall down."

I back away, bump a chair, fumble into it. Put my head down on the table, the smell of onions and 409 greeting me like a friend.

And then his hand is on the back of my neck. Gentle. Brief. The chair opposite scuffs the floor and Ray lets out a little oomph as he sits down. "I'm not going to ask anything of you, Kel. You don't owe me a thing."

Kel. I'm facing away from him with a sideways view of the front door where there's only bleak darkness except for the windmill generators up on the hill beyond the highway, gleaming in a strand of moonlight. Some kind of small truck passes. Then a sedan slows, scatters gravel, then speeds away. I haven't flicked off the neon.

I lift my head enough to turn it toward him, keeping it close to the table.

"You left me," isn't what I meant to say, but these are the words that come from my mouth. "I don't want you back."

63

"I figured that."

"I don't want Beth hurt."

"I won't hurt her."

As I lift my head, he sits up too. I say, "I make the rules."

"Okay."

"You have to earn it, the right to see her. Know her."

"Okay."

"Where you going to stay?"

"Up at my dad's, I guess, if he'll let me."

"He'll let you. But you can't see Beth yet. Not until I tell you."

"Okay."

"You're going to have to earn it. I mean it."

"I know."

"It may take a long, long time."

"Kelly, that's all I got now, is time."

I straighten, thinking, let him go up to his dad's and settle in tonight. Let his dad ask him why he looks so old, so worn out.

I shut off the neon and send him out the door. Go back into Donnie's office to get my purse and the keys to lock up the diner. Catch my face in the Pabst Blue Ribbon mirror over the desk. I'm no longer the girl in the hot red dress.

He's a ways down the highway when I pull up next to him. Tell him to get in the car.

"I don't want nothing from you, Kel."

"Just get in."

We don't talk. He stares at his hands on his knees; I watch the broken yellow line in my headlights.

I drop him at the gravel driveway to his dad's place. He says, "Thank you" and climbs out.

I grip the wheel, then hear myself saying, "Ray."

He stops, leans in. "I'm not asking for nothing."

*

Down the darkened highway and past the stoplight, I have time to consider what has happened and what I want. It's Beth's pointed chin and serious eyes I see in my head, her bending over in jeans and too-small t-shirt, wiping down counters in the diner at fifteen.

Outside my mother's unlit house, I leave the car running, both doors open, the smells of exhaust following me up the walk. My key slips smoothly into the lock, and once inside, I smile at my mother's rasping snore. I stuff hidden money into my pockets and slip into my daughter's room, wake her gently, and with a finger to my lips, whisk her outside and into the car.

"What's happened?" Beth yawns her confusion as she curls up in the back seat.

"We're going on a little adventure."

"What about Grandma?"

"We'll see her soon. Now go back to sleep."

She does, and I drive out of the Nevada desert into an early dawn toward the Rockies where spruce and pine hold their lushness even as hard snow slams down from a pure white sky, where history doesn't repeat itself and no one asks for nothing.

# Complicit

The front door slams. Walls shake. A vase of tasseled wheat slides through my hands onto the kitchen floor. Glass shards lie among stalks as late afternoon sun spills gold onto gold, and I hear his boots in the hall.

A shock of hot wind rattles the screen of the open back door. I glance out. The barn isn't far, a haven if I would only move. But I don't. I wait.

He bursts in, shirt flaked with grime, jeans mud-glazed. He stops when he sees me. Between us, a curl of pleasure, eyes locked, breath vanished.

I step toward him in bare feet, feel the bite of glass, reach up to place a hand on his cheek.

"You're still here," he says.

"Where would I go?"

"I didn't want you here. Not for this." He loops me with thick arms, pulls me close, my ear pressed hard against his farmer's sweat. We stand like vine and tree till he leans down and puts his lips to mine.

When the world comes back, he says, "Where is he?"

If I'd gone to the barn to hide or if I'd left in the wagon as we'd planned, I would not be here to say these words, but I am. "In the field by the creek."

He sets me on a kitchen stool. "Stay." At the door he turns back, his mouth grim.

Linoleum, my toe, the rod my feet rest on, smeared with blood. The quiet slap of the screen door. An owl's hoot from the nearby copse.

I wait in a warm shaft of light, hands in my lap, until I hear a quick loud crack from the north where my husband rides his tractor bare-headed through the wheat.

# Secrets I Tell Myself in Dreams

## At Fourteen

The altar boy inches along the mahogany railing, gold communion plate steady in his hands, blond hair longer than most clean-cut boys wear. He gets away with it somehow, an athlete, a good student, from a big Catholic family with more altar boys to come. He is just who I imagine Ricky Nelson would be if Ricky Nelson could be an altar boy. I don't get away with anything. Boys with buzz cuts and boys with curls to their collars don't see me. This altar boy doesn't see me either, a girl filled with longing, kneeling as still as I can, wearing my floppy straw hat, head slightly turned so I can watch him. And then, because this is a dream, he is kissing me with his tongue inside my mouth, his consecrated hands – or are they just blessed? – gently grasping my neck, thumbs along my jaw, my insides dissolving into holy water. We are in church, we are at the communion rail, I am kneeling in front of God, and I am only thinking of him and his lips and his tongue and his fingers pressing the back of my neck, his thumbs on my throat, a rapture between my legs.

## At Forty-Five

Thin shards of light cut between the boards of the ancient barn revealing dusty rafters. In the front, a loft, heavy with hay, rests on the crossbeams and in the back, the roof soars above the joists, a dark vault, a cathedral of sorts. Thick rope hangs down. Filaments of hemp shine in a slender bar of sun. And beneath that bar are hands, my hands, tied at the end of rope, wrists chafed, bone ripping from bone, body suspended above the dirt floor. Shoulders ache, triceps ache, feet fill with blood. When I wake, I search for bruising.

## Last Night

As if life were a game of Mario Cart, stuck in animated worlds with cartoon cars and cruiser bikes, princesses and Donkey Kong, surrounded by colors fully saturated, my nether self flashes through mining shafts, fiery castles, and shopping malls, hurtles into sheds on the sides of mountains, careens down glistening blue and white slopes, chases through deep space on a rainbow highway where the slightest misstep flings me into blackness. But if this were waking life, the game would put me back on track, allow me to win or lose. In the dream, I go on forever spinning mud, running into bats, and killing cows, inked, shrunk, blasted, and shelled, no finish line in sight.

# She Can't Say No

The wait for a table at Houston's is an hour-and-a-half. Smokers sit along the rim of the koi pond outside, while Matt and his girlfriend crowd into the bar with everyone else. He's been hanging out with Anna for a few weeks, so when his old buddy Kerrick threads his way over and gives him a friendly punch in the arm, Matt doesn't hesitate to introduce them.

"I know you," says Kerrick, smiling into Anna's almost perfect face, almost because there is a tiny scar lifting from lip to nostril.

"You do?" Anna swings her foot and sips her dirty martini.

Matt thinks, wait a minute. "How do you know each other?" He leans between Anna on her bar stool and Kerrick who's standing too close.

"Around," says Anna and brushes Matt's cheek. The stroke reassures him, but he won't make this mistake again, no more introducing Anna to any more friends. He should have known better. She's clearly out of his league. He knows it, everyone knows it, but still, she's here. With him.

"Matt? Party of two?" The hostess in her black dress and high heels hovers.

He takes Anna's elbow, steers her away, grimaces at his friend. "See ya, Kerrick."

Anna says, "See ya, Kerrick," her eyes lingering for the briefest of seconds on Kerrick's lips. Matt squeezes her arm.

Once the waiter leaves them alone at the table, Matt asks Anna how she knows his friend, a fast-track kind of guy, gel in his hair and Hugo Boss shoes.

"I met him once." When she smiles, the scar on her upper lip whitens. Sometimes when Matt wakes up in the morning, alone, thinking of her, the word "harelip" pops into his brain. He's hinted to her about childhood operations, bringing up tonsillectomies, appendectomies, avoiding the strange medical term for the kind of surgery he looked up on Wikipedia, but she never answers him, always too busy teasing him about his cowlick or his choice of socks. Looking at her mouth now, he can almost feel its slight ridge on his tongue. He coughs. "And?"

"And what?"

"You were flirting with him."

"I know." And she rubs the side of her naked foot along Matt's calf and tucks it behind his knee. "I'm sorry."

Later, up in her apartment on the second floor, after he's taken the opportunity to kiss every one of her various ridges, clefts, and valleys, he flops on his back and stares at the light fixture, suctioned like a flying saucer to the ceiling, shimmering in the faint yellow cast from the street lamp. He knows she's going to hurt him. He needs to give her up. Now. Climb out of bed and leave. Guys are always doing that. Why can't he? But then she rolls into him, snuggling her head beneath his arm.

He remembers their first date, a blind one arranged by a co-worker, Anna coming up behind him to press her breasts into his back at the Huntington Library ticket counter. Shocking him, yes, but he found he liked being shocked. How could he not? His only other girlfriend lived down the street for most of his twenty-two years. They'd never even slept together.

71

That first date at the Huntington, Matt led Anna into the Japanese garden where, across from the steep lacquered bridge, three men on ladders were applying fake cherry blossoms to the branches of a huge tree.

"Must be a movie," he'd said.

Anna placed palms and fingers together in front of her chest and bowed. "I could be your geisha," she whispered. Her eyes flicked up to his, then down, but not before he caught her lips spreading into a smile, her scar a white tattoo. She pulled him behind the teahouse into a forest of bamboo and he made love to her on the spongy carpet of moss while the murmur of voices, laughter, and the occasional shout, melted away like snow.

But even then he'd wondered, just as he does now, his body wrapped around hers, snug inside her deep burgundy sheets, if all this binding together, the two of them, means the same to her as it does to him.

Ignoring the loan applications stacked on his desk, Matt calls Kerrick. "I want to know if there's something between you and Anna." He tries to sound casual, but his voice carries a tinge of anger.

"What? You really like her or something?" asks Kerrick.

"Or something."

"Look, we met at a party. Nothing to it."

"Nothing?"

"Never saw her after that one night. Too bad. She's hot."

"You slept with her?"

"Did I say that?"

"No, but you did sleep with her."

"Dude, I'm sorry, but, you know, she can't say no."

Matt parks across the street from Anna's apartment letting the darkness envelop him. Her windows are black, her porch light glows like a cigarette.

It's been two days since he's seen her. He hasn't called, hasn't returned her calls to him. He shouldn't be here, but he can't stay away. He needs a glimpse of her, just one, before he calls it quits.

When he falls asleep in the cramped bucket seat of his car, he dreams he's at work. An elderly woman opens a checking account while Anna, hidden beneath his desk, busies herself with his zipper. He struggles to keep the grin off his face, but can't. The bank manager, an ex-basketball player, skinny, and balding, stomps over and lifts the desk into the air. Everyone in the bank – tellers, customers, the security guard – circle the two of them and chant, "She can't say no, she can't say no, she can't –"

A hard rapping on the car window startles him awake, his head knocking glass, his right leg tangled around the stick shift.

Anna, her face cupped between her hands, peers in. "Is that you?"

"No," he mumbles, unfolding himself and pushing open the door.

She laughs, and when he steps out of the car, she drapes her arms around his neck, presses her body hard against his, looks up at him. "Are you stalking me?"

Kneading the night air, he tries to keep his hands away. "No ... yes. I don't know."

"Why haven't you called me back?"

He reaches up to remove her arms, but the heat from her skin coaxes his fingers down the small of her back. He kisses her damaged lip, slow and gentle as if she were a bride.

# Doing Mr. Velvet

All the dead bodies end up in Riverside County, and my cousin Emma tells me one more won't matter. We're on the I-10, slipping over the San Bernardino-Riverside line, Emma up ahead in Mr. Velvet's gold Cadillac DeVille, Mr. V. dead in the trunk. I'm following behind in the station wagon.

We're not bad people, Emma and I, and she says it's our destiny – as cousins from a long line of beauticians – to open our own day spa. And now that it's possible, we've worked too hard to waste time going to court to prove my innocence. And since she's *Mrs.* Velvet and the sole heir to Mr. Velvet's House of Hair in the event of his death, she doesn't want to draw any unnecessary attention to herself. If anyone asks, Harold Warren Velvet went to Vegas.

Emma turns onto a two-lane highway for a couple of miles and then onto a gravel road. It's dark, and as lonely as a hair salon on Monday mornings, the clouds around the moon reminding me of our grandma's spit-curls.

An abrupt thump from behind, a voice at my ear: "For all have sinned and fall short of the glory of God."

I scream and jerk the steering wheel. In the rear view mirror is Jesus himself, all riveting eyes and bearded chin.

The wagon sways and bumps along the side of the road, spewing sand and grit. I don't throw up; I pee my pants.

"Gilly?"

Shit. The Almighty knows my name.

The reek of fries and heavy sweat helps me calm down. I know this smell. It belongs to Holy Roller, the guy who preaches in the middle of the intersection of Baseline and Haven back in Rancho Cucamonga. We met my second day in California where I came to learn the family trade. He was digging through the dumpster out back and said to me, "I used to be in the Truth and now I'm not. I've accepted Jesus Christ as my personal savior." I bought him a couple Whoppers and have been feeding him ever since.

"What the hell are you doing in Emma's station wagon?" I ask him now.

"Hiding from the cops." He starts to slide between the bucket seats and into the front and I swat him back. Emma's gonna be hotter than an uncertified curling iron about this new development.

Emma's taillights flash red across Holy's bearded face. "Is that Mr. Velvet up there?"

"Keep your head down!"

We've caught up to the Cadillac, its bumper recognizable, so I hit the brakes, fishtailing a little, to fall behind. Emma's not gonna like having a witness to our crime.

Before long she turns off the road and into squishy sand. The clouded moon turns the yucca trees into bandits, the boulders into bears. Emma parks the DeVille on a ridge of rocks. We are finally in the middle of nowhere.

"Holy," I say. "Emma can't know you're here. You gotta stay in the wagon and be quiet, you understand? I mean it."

"Fear not, little flock."

A long gulch stretches below the ridge, willows on both sides. When I reach Emma, I lean against the Caddie's front grille to keep from shaking too hard.

"Don't wimp out on me now, Gilly. It's your neck, don't forget."

"But I didn't mean to do it."

75

"No one's gonna believe that now, so let's get this car in the gully and light it up."

She's right, of course. Emma's always right, and yet . . .

I glance over my shoulder at the station wagon. It's still dark and quiet.

Mr. Velvet started to go stiff back at Mr. Velvet's House of Hair while Emma made a plan. By the time we were ready to leave, we had to wrestle him into the trunk and now we have to wrestle him out. We tug and pull and finally get him onto the sand. Emma said we'd put him in the driver's seat because then it would look like he decided to ramble through the desert for god-only-knows-what-reason, and something went terribly wrong, but his body still won't bend, so we just slide him in along the front seat.

"That Mr. Velvet in there?" Holy Roller. Popping up next to me.

"Gilly," snaps Emma.

"I didn't ask him to come."

"Dammit." Emma swings around and glares at Holy. "Don't screw with me, Jesus-freak. Gilly's in trouble and I'm helping her out. You go wait in the station wagon, you hear? You lay down and you don't look. I don't wanna hurt you."

He says softly, "Take my yoke upon you and learn of me, for I am meek and —"

Emma grabs him by the arm and drags him back to the wagon, me hurrying behind, explaining to Holy what happened. "It was an accident. I was washing Mr. Velvet's hair —"

"You don't have to explain anything to the likes of him!" shouts Emma.

"But I didn't murder Mr. Velvet. I was washing his hair —"

"Shut up, Gil —"

"He jumped up when I sprayed him with hot water and then he slipped —"

"Stop it, you stupid, stupid girl."

"And hit his head." I'm hanging my own head.

Emma lets go of Holy when we reach her station wagon. He glances from Emma to me and back to Emma, looking just like Jesus does in pictures of him chasing the money-changers out of the temple. He says, "So when you put the plastic over his face, Emma, you were helping him?"

Her body stiffens. "What plastic, you idiot?"

He wipes his nose on his sleeve. "Well, I was hungry so I was looking for Gilly through your window. And when Mr. Velvet moved, you covered his face with Saran wrap. I saw the box. You held it there until he stopped moving."

These are the most words I've heard him say except when he quotes the Bible. It takes me a second to get it, then I gape at Emma, my cousin and life-long best friend. "You killed him and you were gonna let me think I –"

"Don't believe this junkie, Gilly."

Fumbling for the wagon keys in my pocket, I haul Holy to the passenger door. Open it.

"Where are you going?" Emma comes after us, grips my shoulder.

I shrug her off, yell at Holy to get in and shut the door. He does. Emma tries to hold onto me, but I throw an elbow into her chest, and she slips in the sand.

I race around the car, jump into the driver's seat, lock doors. She's there, hammering on the roof, peering in the window, her hair mussed, her face violet with rage.

I slam the accelerator. The wheels churn sand, then shoot us forward. We hit the black top hard, and Holy Roller says to me, "I am the resurrection, and the life: he that believeth in me, though he were dead, yet shall live."

It isn't until we spy the first billboard for the International House of Pancakes, and Holy Roller mutters something about Whoppers, that I roll down the window and poke my head into the cool dawn. Behind us, at the foot of the mountains, I see a rod of smoke twisting to the sky.

77

Emma, if nothing else, is a practical woman. Somehow she's managed to light up Mr. Velvet in his Cadillac crypt, sticking to her plan. And if I know Emma, and I guess now I do, that means she's not going to let anything or anyone stand in the way of her transformation of Mr. Velvet's House of Hair into Emma Elkins' European Day Spa, and someone else is going to have to take the blame for doing Mr. Velvet.

I turn to Holy Roller. "What do you say we take a vacation?"

"Jesus spent 40 days in the desert, didn't he?"

"I'll take that as a yes."

# The Way It Can Be

Josh fired a blunt, sucked it down, and exhaled a borealis of smoke. A trick, she thought as he moved on her, his hands pirating her breasts, her belly, her legs, between her legs; him constructing crystal edifices; her fingers stretched taut in search of sparklers, prism splinters, clusters of coincidence.

# Chalk Dust

Most hot June days the artist draws 3-D pictures on the sidewalk with colored pastels. Staircases are his specialty, winding down down down, spiraling into the earth, giving way to charcoal abysses. These stone steps appear so real you have to repress the urge to stoop and lay a finger to the rich ochres, the somber browns, the deep umbers to make certain your eyes are, indeed, deceiving you.

When you slip off a flip-flop and use your toe to smear the crack in the top step that leads down into the first sub-basement of today's carefully wrought masterpiece, you could swear in the instant before the artist shoos you away, that you feel a falling away in the sidewalk, a vacuum beneath your foot, the tongue of dark air against your ankle.

So you retreat and watch the artist drop onto his hands and knees and with his shallow tray of crumbling colors, repair the damage you've done. Yet you don't remember the solidity of concrete against your toe, the sensation of powdery chalk, only their absence, the promise of descent.

You lean over to scrutinize the bottom of your toe. It's skin-pink. You glance along the gray concrete toward the artist who is standing now, his t-shirt stained in the dusty hues of his magnificent masterpiece.

*

Later, after the night sky becomes a pit of black, when everyone has gone home to their last glasses of red wine, their cool sheets, the warm concaves of their girlfriends' bodies, you return to the staircase that gleams under the street lamp. With only the slightest of second thoughts, you place your foot firmly on the uppermost step and find yourself descending. A certain glee rushes through your blood as the light from above begins to fade.

A few moments later, a maintenance man moves out of the shadows, hosing down the sidewalks, spraying water in a gentle arc over the staircase, watching as the artist's chalk lifts slowly on a liquid tide and flows away, leaving behind nothing but damp cement.

# Kindling

Packs of Kents wedged between the windshield and dash of the Plymouth, Mom and Dad lighting one smoke after another, puffing away, the radio on low, spitting static. The Mojave Desert barreled by outside, long and wide and hot.

Dad bought a cooler from Sears for the trip. It straddled the hump in the front seat under the butt-filled ashtray. Air from the vents was supposed to chill the car by flowing over the ice in the cooler. Me in the backseat, I never once experienced a wisp of cold.

Nothing but sand between us and The Alamo, and two hours out of L.A., I dripped sweat, my eyes burning from smoker's smog. I cranked down the window and stuck my head and shoulders out, face to the wind, my hair a yellow hurricane.

Mom hollered over the seat, "Roll that window up, Sheri. You're letting in all the hot air."

"But it's like Death Valley back here."

Mom jabbed the red tip of her cigarette at me. "Don't sass."

I flopped back onto the itchy cloth upholstery, put my bare feet against the hot glass of the window, and watched the blur of red rock and blue sky through the pane, thinking about my friends back home at the beach slathered in baby-oil, going to the movies, meeting boys. Their dads sold insurance or drilled teeth or remodeled houses while mine taught American history and believed I'd grow up stupid if we didn't take a road trip every summer and "steep ourselves in the rich and edifying tapestry that is – THE PAST."

What about the present? What about *my* present? Dissipating with every mile.

He was jabbering about Davy Crockett and the Alamo siege. I couldn't see Mom, but knew she was thumbing her cigarette filter like she always did. I took out the matchbook hidden in my pocket, tore a cardboard stick, and struck it. Played with the flame, slid my finger into the silky yellow part until the match burned down. I didn't make a sound.

We stopped at a rest area to pee and empty the ashtrays. I was the first one out and into the smack of heat. "Ugh."

Mom followed, stretching and yawning, smoke wisping from her mouth.

Dad slammed the car door and made a flourish toward the scrub brush.

"Oh, ye pioneers," he said in his deep declaiming voice, "It is 1836 and you, Sheri, are traveling west –"

I couldn't help myself. "Then Sheri's been traveling the wrong way, Dad."

He cleared his throat, took a drag on his cigarette, and kept talking. "Traveling west in a Conestoga wagon wearing a calico bonnet and a homemade dress of wool –"

I shook my head and slouched my way down the steaming asphalt path toward the concrete facility, knowing Dad couldn't really know what he was talking about. Wool in this heat!

The restroom was dim and smelly, but almost not-hot.

"That you, Sheri?" Mom called from the stall.

"It ain't Marilyn Monroe."

83

"Don't say 'ain't' and go back to the car and get the sandwiches and the jar of ice tea."

"I have to pee."

"I'll be done by the time you get back. They're in the front seat in a paper bag. There's a table in some shade on the side of the building." I could still hear her talking as I cut through the sand toward the car, then she called out, "Sheri, are you listening to me? Sheri?"

The metal handle stung my fingers. I yelped, growled. The handle felt hotter than the match flame. Unbuttoning the bottom of my shirt, I used it as a potholder and opened the car door.

I coughed at the foul air inside the Plymouth and snatched the paper sack, then caught a whiff of something burning. The tip of a cigarette must have fallen off because a glowing ball of ash and tobacco smoldered in the seat cushion. I watched it nibble at the frayed upholstery, couldn't take my eyes off its angry redness. A gust of wind whooshed past and into the car. A lick of fire shot up. My heart thumped. I reached for the ice tea jar, the glass warm in my hand.

I could have twisted open the lid, dowsed the hot little blaze, but I turned away instead, hesitating for a moment before deliberately striding from the car, across the sand, glancing over my shoulder only after I reached the picnic table. It looked so normal, the vivid sky, the flat endless highway, the car door yawning open to let the breeze clear out the reek of cigarette. I smiled. Let it burn.

"Sheri, hurry up. We're hungry." Mom sat with her back to me, twisting around, her cig bouncing between her lips while Dad stood on the edge of the rest area, a thread of smoke snaking from his right hand, gazing out at nothing but scrub and rock.

# Body-Snatching

My mother's refuge was the dining room table where she sewed most evenings, fabric skittering under the needle. I leaned over and whispered, "I'm leaving."

She frowned at my mini-skirt, but all she said was, "Be good."

The air outside was jasmine-scented. Kids played kickball at the end of the cul-de-sac. Cars rumbled down the busy road behind our houses.

It was Mr. Porter who opened the door. "There you are, Lizzie, right on time."

His warm blue eyes made me blush. I dipped around him to get inside, feeling heat from his body, both glad and ashamed I'd washed and set my hair — as if I'd done it for him.

"Still planning on going to Berkeley?" he asked.

"Yes sir."

"Not going to be a hippie? Join the SDS?"

"My dad would kill me."

"That's a good girl." Mr. Porter rested his hand on my shoulder. My body tingled as I turned and his fingers fell away. I knew he was watching me.

Debi and Todd waited in the family room, Monopoly set up on the maple coffee table.

The Porters came in to say good-bye and Debi rushed them for kisses. Todd, twelve, aloof, in his view too old to be baby-sat, stayed on the sofa, sorting the stacks of blue and pink and yellow money. I waved. Mr. Porter looked a little like Troy Donahue, just older. Mrs. Porter was no Sandra Dee.

After we finished the Monopoly game – Todd won – we made popcorn and cocoa and watched *Gunsmoke*, me in the middle with Debi in rainbow pajamas on one side and Todd in plaid PJs on the other.

Debi said, "Isn't Miss Kitty pretty? I want a cat name."

I said, "We could call you Puss."

"No way. Puss in Boots is a boy!"

*Gunsmoke* ended with Marshall Dillon saving Dodge City from home-brewed TNT and I watched Debi brush her teeth and tucked her in. When I got back to the family room, Todd was engrossed in a black-and-white sci-fi movie on TV.

"You seen this before?" he asked as I sat down next to him on the sofa.

I shook my head, put my feet on the coffee table. "What's happened so far?"

"All these people in this town are crazy, going around saying their mother isn't their mother or their brother isn't their brother." Todd pointed toward the television. "He's the main guy. He's a doctor."

We watched as the doctor and his friends stood around a giant peapod on a pool table. The pod cracked open, revealing something waxy and half formed inside, with a face like a mannequin.

"What is that?" asked Todd.

"I think it's a person."

Todd moved closer to me and when more giant pods were discovered in the doctor's greenhouse, he latched onto my hand and squeezed. His fingers were strong and hot and damp. I didn't make him let go.

By the time the characters on the screen figured out aliens were trying to steal their emotions, Todd's shoulder was pressed against my arm, his hip near mine, our legs touching each other. His warmth seeped through my skin, carrying a tiny electric current along my arms, into my chest, my stomach, places that surprised me. He gripped my hand, or I gripped his, both of us hanging on at each twist in the story.

The doctor and his girlfriend were running away from town. She was exhausted and wanted to lie down, but the doctor wouldn't let her.

Todd's eyes were glued to the TV, his thumb rubbing my palm. I grabbed his thumb, held it tight.

The doctor dragged her along, yelled at her, begged her to stay awake, and then for a moment and only a moment, he looked away, and when he turned back, she'd fallen asleep. It didn't take long for her to change into a pod person.

The doctor raved along the highway, stopping traffic, a lunatic, but no one listened to him until two trucks collided and their cargoes of hundreds of pods spilled across the blacktop.

Todd's fingers, my fingers, clasped together on my thigh at the hem of my mini-skirt. I pulled his hand across my skin, sucked in air, shivered with the sudden ache between my legs.

I felt his eyes on me and dropped his hand, stood up fast, not looking at him.

"That was scary, wasn't it?" I rushed into the kitchen, opened the fridge door. He followed me, stood next to me, boy feet poking out from under his pajamas. My face burned in spite of the refrigerated air. My whole body burned.

"Lizzie?" His voice was soft and rough.

"You want a Coke?" I asked, not taking my eyes off an uncovered pork chop on a shelf.

"Now? Before *bed?*"

"Why not?" I poked the milk carton, flicked at a package of bologna.

"Mom says —"

"It's okay, Todd. Just this once." I handed him the Coke bottle, then moved the boysenberry jam next to the milk, the mayonnaise jar to the other side.

"You don't think there could be pods like that, do you?"

"Nope. No way." I shut the fridge door and wiped my hands on the towel hanging from the handle. "Now be a good boy and go to bed."

"Lizzie?"

I looked up. He held the soda in one hand, the church key in the other, poised to pop the bottle cap. The kitchen light was bright on his somber face, the hall dark behind him, and I noticed the new sharpness to his chin, the blue of his eyes, the movement of an Adam's apple in his throat when he said good-night.

# Between Hay and Grass, 1949

The sons of Joseph Greer wrangled a dozen horses through the open gate as flames crested Hook Mountain. The herd, mostly bays, skittered onto the meadow. Lupine, baneberry, yellow Mexican hat surrendered under hooves. Plumes of smoke tarnished the sky, staining the sun copper. Charley studied the fire near the top of the slope while Luke slid down from the buckskin, and pulling the horse with him, grabbed the wire gate to drag it shut.

"Forget the gate and take that saddle off-a Buck," said Charley, the elder brother at fifteen.

Luke whipped his head around. "He's my horse."

"He'll be safer with the herd."

"You don't know that."

"Horses got natural instincts. Better out there than trapped in our valley."

"What about Moe?"

Charley patted the old cob beneath him. "We might need him."

"No way. Forget it. You can't make me."

Charley bent forward, jaw set. "I can and I will."

"Pa would never make me give him up."

"Pa ain't here, is he?"

Luke's face paled, then went red as he yanked at the cinch and hauled off the saddle, the blanket falling at his feet.

The fire had started up on Big Top two days before. They'd listened to the radio pour out news about how heat

89

and wind urged the flames through aspen, pine, and dry meadow grasses, how firefighters, smokejumpers too, were on the attack. Charley never thought the blaze would spread to Hook Mountain, inching over the ridge into their spruce — his spruce, but it had. Their mother was pregnant, close to term. Twenty-six miles from town meant no phone lines, and though they had a working generator and an old RCA dry-cell radio, Charley and his ma decided they couldn't risk getting cut off from the outside.

Below in the pasture, the horses sniffed the air, their deep red coats sifted with ash. Paulette, the lead mare, nudged them away from the smell of burning timber. Luke's buckskin bobbed his head and whinnied. From below, the other horses answered.

"Go on." The boy shoved at Buck's neck. "Git. Run away with your dumb-old friends." He pitched the bridle at the horse, snatched up the blanket, and threw that. Confused, the buckskin hesitated, then took off.

Old Moe moved forward, but Charley backed him up, saying to Luke, "Fix up the tack like we did this morning." Before taking out the horses, they'd lugged the stable gear from the hay barn into a wide patch of bare ground, covering it with rocks in hopes that the fire, if it came, would jump over. Now Luke threw tack and rocks into a messy pile.

When his brother was finished, Charley leaned from his saddle and offered him a hand. Luke grimaced, but took it and swung up behind him. Down in the meadow Buck and the other horses trotted after Paulette, instinct spurring them on, away from the smoke.

Charley rode Old Moe hard, drawing up in front of the ranch house in a kick of dirt. Pushing himself off the back of the horse, Luke stomped toward the porch and spun around to face his brother, brow furrowed, mouth clenched, before banging inside.

The sound of the old Pontiac's idling engine near the corral made the older boy straighten in his saddle. He'd struggled to get the car started before they took the horses to the gate and been afraid to turn it off, but it was still going. They could leave soon. He dropped to the ground and smoothed his hand along the horse's withers, whispering, "Don't you worry none, you old bag-a-bones. You'll find Paulette and the other horses, won't you?"

The gelding snorted, then his ears twitched and Charley heard the sound of a vehicle rattling up the road.

He walked toward the battered truck as it braked. Rubbed his nose to keep from sneezing and dipped his head to the driver's side window.

"Mr. McNary. Fire ain't got to you yet?"

"Jeez-o, Mary, and Uncle Joe." The big man hauled himself out of the Ford and stared at Hook Mountain. "I come to take you and your ma to town."

"That's okay. I got the Pontiac ready to go."

"You got gas in that thing?"

"Full tank."

"How's your ma holding up? When's she due?"

Charley shifted his feet. McNary was one of those ranchers who spent more time at the Glass Lake Diner flirting with waitresses than working his cows. Pa'd never liked him. Neither did Charley. "Not for a month. She'll be fine. We're all fine."

"You sure, son?" His sharp eyes darted to the house.

"We're leaving in a bit."

"Well, you tell your ma I come by." McNary folded himself back into the driver's seat. Charley turned away, relieved to hear the crunch of tires.

The Pontiac was rusted along the bottom, but Charley loved the long snout of it and the fenders' big curves. He'd been seven or so when Pa brought the car home, just before

Pearl Harbor. It had gleamed like gold under the late afternoon sun, both boys hopping around it, begging for rides, but Ma was mad. A ranch needed a truck. Pa was supposed to use his head. He'd be the ruin of them all. Then he headed off to the Pacific, and Ma moved the boys to town, Pontiac and all.

When Pa came back from the war and they returned to the ranch, Ma drove the Pontiac, Pa his new second-hand pickup. But not too long ago, the truck landed upside down in the reservoir along with the horse trailer, the stallion, and Pa. Pulled out by divers and a heavy crane, his father now rested on a grassy knoll under a fir tree, *Joseph Greer – Beloved Husband and Father* carved into gray stone. Charley wondered how you could really love someone who always let you down, but Ma must've. She got pregnant, didn't she? It had embarrassed him, his folks too old to have a baby, too old to – for any of that. And now Pa was gone.

Charley twisted around to view the mountain. The fire was working its way through the trees, smoke twisting off their tops. He climbed into the car, and slamming the door hard, drove up to the ranch house.

Ma held open the screen. "Luke's gone."

Charley's throat tightened. "Gone where?"

"After Buck. You know how he loves that horse."

He looked away from Ma, not wanting her to see his anger. He mumbled, "Paulette will take the herd down Elk Creek away from the fire. He'll know that."

"Don't make it worse by yelling at him."

"Well, I won't whoop him."


At the far gate, the rocks around Buck's saddle were scattered, the bridle and reins gone. Luke's just like Pa, Charley thought. Buying the Pontiac instead of the truck they needed. Buying Ma pearls when the barn's roof needed fixing. Getting them so deep in debt they had to sell the stallion. *His* stallion, not Luke's, but his.

He loped over the meadow, slowing only when he entered the trees, picking his way down a rocky slant. The horses wouldn't have gone too far and as soon as they felt safe, they would stop to graze along the creek. On Hook Mountain, fire chewed away at the forest, the wind lifting flames, igniting smaller hot spots.

Buck stood in a rocky clearing. The horse wore the bridle and reins. No rider. Charley stood in his stirrups, surveying the tall grass. Then, on a slight incline, he spied Luke sprawled on his back, not moving.

"Luke!" Charley raced to his brother, dismounted fast. "You okay?"

"I could be dead for all you care."

"Well, you ain't, are you?" Charley took off his hat and crouched closer.

"Leave me be, will you?"

"So you got thrown, huh?" Charley leaned over to help, but Luke punched him square in the nose. The unexpected pain bent Charley in half, hands on knees, dizzy and furious enough to fall on Luke, pinning his shoulders.

Luke squirmed. "Get off-a me." He worked his fist close to Charley's stomach, but had no leverage. He thrashed and kicked, tears rolling down his dirty face.

Charley didn't move. "Why do you do stuff like that?"

Luke stopped struggling, staring hard at his brother, and said, "You're crying."

Charley clambered up and seized the reins around Old Moe's neck, causing the horse to back away and rear. "Damn it. Don't you understand we gotta get Ma out of here?"

"Buck is my horse. Pa gave him to me."

Charley swung around hard. "He gave me the stallion and that didn't mean a damn thing, did it?"

Both brothers growled. The horses tramped the ground, snorted. A bird lifted into smoky air, and Charley turned and saw a lick of flame off to the left.

His nose smarted from the blow. He wiped the blood away with his sleeve. Then Luke nodded and Charley nodded too and without another word, they mounted up.

They returned the horses to the corral, Luke heading into the house to bring out their belongings while Charley checked the Pontiac's gas gauge. The tank was full, as full as before.

"Open the trunk," hollered Luke from the porch.

The car key was in the ignition, the trunk key dangling from a chain. When Charley finally got it open, chain and trunk key dropped to the floor. He reached under the seat, felt around, and pulled out a half empty pack of Camels along with the key. Pa's smokes. An image of his father came to him, working a skittish young horse, his voice soothing, his hand gentle, a cigarette hanging from his mouth. He slipped one into his shirt pocket and tucked the rest back under the seat.

When they were finished packing the car, Charley said to Luke, "You're gonna have to ride Buck, and I guess we'll take Moe too. You'll have to lead him."

"I don't mind."

"Then go get them."

Luke ran to the corral and Charley spied Ma on the porch. He sprang up the stairs and took her arm. It felt hot and damp.

Ma said, "I see Luke fought back when you tried to whoop him."

"He started it, not me."

"I don't doubt that for a minute. Oh, I forgot the sandwiches inside."

"Let me get you to the car and I'll go get 'em."

Charley licked mustard from a knife and placed it in the kitchen sink; then grabbing the towel that held their lunch, he paused to look around, the horsehair sofa, the steep steps to the loft where he and Luke slept, the round oak table, Pa's chair. He tried to imagine all this, his home – their home – charred and broken by fire, but couldn't do it. Wouldn't do it.

Outside, the flames were camped half way down the mountain, trees shivering in the smoky air, and at the base, Charley caught the glint of water as the creek curved in and out. Pa had named it after Ma, and Charley prayed Katie Creek would be enough to stand against the fire.

"Hey, thought you were in a hurry." It was Luke riding Buck, Old Moe on a lead line behind him.

They got as far as the bend in the road, a half a mile or so, when the Pontiac choked to a stop, the sun slanting smudgy orange through the windshield glass.

Charley climbed out and opened the hood.

Ma rolled down her window. "What's wrong?"

"I don't know."

"Can we push it? Pop the clutch?"

He looked at her. "Who? You, me, and Luke?"

"I can steer," she said.

"If she says she can do it, why the heck not?" asked Luke, tying the horses to a pine sapling. Ma slid awkwardly to the driver's side. She barely fit.

The narrow road curved around a shear of rock on the right and a weedy gully on the left. The boys, on either side of the car, inched the sedan ahead of them. The day's heat pressed, the air bitter. They pushed, building momentum,

Charley suddenly feeling the car give under his hands, but then he realized it wasn't following the bend in the road.

"Turn the wheel right. Ma. Turn the wheel!"

The Pontiac braked and stopped. Charley stumbled, but caught himself and rushed forward. The front left wheel hung over the lip of the ditch. "Put on the emergency brake. Stay there. The car's okay, but there's not much room."

Ma turned toward them, her face white, her brown eyes calm. "It's starting."

Charley said, "It's not starting, Ma. We —"

"My water just broke," she said. "The baby's coming."

"How can that be?"

His ma shrugged. "I guess this baby got impatient."

They knew about birth, they were ranch kids, but this was different. This was their ma. The walk from the car to the house took longer than Charley could have imagined, Ma leaning first on Charley, then on Luke. She assured them they had time. They stopped only once for a contraction, Charley, tight-mouthed, not knowing how to comfort her, Luke wanting to make a chair with their arms and carry her. Ma barked, "I can very well walk."

Charley stole looks at the mountain where the fire burned across the slope, inching down, sending up great curls of smoke. When they were almost to the house, Ma said, her voice uneven, "You'd think that good-for-nothing McNary would've come to see if we needed help."

Charley almost blurted out the old rancher had been by, but with a blush of shame, he bit his tongue.

They got her settled into her bed. She had another contraction and when it was over, she said, "This could go on for a while. Where's the fire now?"

"I'll go and check."

She lay back against the pillow and closed her eyes.

The brothers slipped outside where the air hung thick and still. Above, the flames burned slowly. Charley told Luke to turn the generator back on.

Luke stepped in close, whispered, "Lemme go get help."

"What'd you mean?"

"I can ride Buck into town, get someone to come get Ma."

Charley grit his teeth. *He* was the one who was supposed to know exactly what to do and all he'd done was mess up, sending McNary away, upsetting Luke about his damn horse, making Ma worry about his brother taking off, and then, *then*, letting the damn car run out of gas because he was pretty sure now that's what he'd done, and the part that scared him the most was not saying anything about how the tank might be empty, and then almost pushing the car into the ditch with Ma in it. He was no better than Pa. Worse than Pa.

"Charley, can I go or not?"

Fingering the cigarette in his shirt pocket, Charley said, "It's getting dark and who knows where else the fire is. It could be across the road somewhere."

"But I could do it. Buck and I could go."

"What if something happened to you? Ma would never forgive me."

"I'm as good a rider as you."

"Not saying you're not, but, damn it, Luke, I need you. Anyway, I don't think you can go that far and get back in time. Please, just turn on that generator so Ma can have some light."

Luke clomped down the steps, but Charley stopped him, saying, "Don't go running off on me, Luke. I mean it. I need you."

Luke called over his shoulder, "Ain't going nowhere."

Charley pulled the cigarette from his shirt pocket. Rolled it between his fingers, put it to his nose to smell, and stared up at the glowing mountain, not thinking about Luke or Ma or the baby, but about Pa, teasing Ma as she hung up their jeans to dry, showing Luke how to use a rope, clapping Charley on the shoulder after a high school football game, knowing Charley wished he could play, but was needed on the ranch. Charley sighed wearily, too tired to be angry anymore, at least for now.

They were on the porch watching the flames creep down the mountain when she cried out for them. Her room was airless. She lay panting and sweating on the bed, her knees pulled up with the sheet over them. "Third baby's fast. Where's Luke?"

Charley gently smoothed hair from her face. "Getting some towels to clean up the mess."

"You sound like you know what you're doing," she said.

"I sound like a rancher."

The word "wait" came out Ma's mouth as a gulp, her face contorting. He waited.

"Oh," she said when she could breathe. "Hurry, Char – ow-ow."

He grabbed the sheet and looked beneath, then shut his eyes. Another moan from Ma and Charley opened his eyes. Saw what was happening. Urgency cleared his head. A baby was coming. He moved forward, his hands reaching out for the red circle between her legs

Ma said, "Just – hold the – don't pull – let it come – to you."

The soft head was wet in his hands, covered in blood, but to his amazement, he recognized a forehead, two slits above a tiny nose.

"Keep – one hand on – head –"

Charley saw the shoulder. It was caught. He reached forward, hesitating a bit, then slid his finger inside his mother and moved her skin aside to create space for the baby.

Ma pushed one last time. A groan came from the doorway. Luke.

Charley yelled, "Bring me that towel." And the boy did.

One shoulder was out, another coming, and then Charley almost lost hold of the tiny, slippery being, but Luke pressed against it lightly with the towel, and Charley held on.

Ma gasped, "The cord, Charley."

Luke answered, "I'll get scissors."

"A girl, Ma. It's a girl," whispered Charley.

Luke came back with sturdy kitchen shears. Charley gave him a nod and the younger boy snipped the cord.

Ma said, "Wipe her nose. Get the mucus out."

"With the towel?"

"Use your fingers – careful."

Charley wiped his hands on the towel and did what needed to be done. The baby let out a wail.

"Bring her to me." Ma held out her arms.

He asked, "She's okay?"

His mother made an inspection and said, "Oh, she's beautiful. So little, but beautiful."

Charley and Luke grinned.

*

After a while, the brothers ambled out on the porch to check the fire. The flames on the mountain formed a slender thread of scarlet through the spruce, the night air calm as well water.

"No wind. We should be okay for now. You did good in there." Charley could still feel the tingly warmth of the baby's small head on his hands.

"You too."

"We'll head out first light."

Catching his brother's eye, nodding, Luke said, "Whatever you say."


Charley woke to the drone of an engine. Beyond the window, a breeze ruffled through the trees. The blaze was kicking up three-quarters of the way down the mountain. Luke sprawled on the other bed, asleep. Below, the baby cried. Still wearing his clothes from the previous day, he plucked the cigarette from his shirt pocket, stashed it behind his ear, and climbed down the ladder-like stairs.


"What's that in your hair?" Ma was sitting up in bed, the baby hidden beneath the blanket, nursing.

"One of Pa's smokes," he said and touched it, feeling lighter – almost giddy – for the first time since his father died.

Luke pushed into the room. "What are we gonna name her?"

"Josephine," said Charley without hesitation. "After Pa."

Ma looked at him and then at Luke. "Josephine?"

They both grinned and then laughed. Josephine's mouth was a tiny "O" amidst the blankets.

They heard it at the same time, another plane in the distance. Luke rushed to the window.

"It's them!" he shouted. "Smoke-jumpers coming. Can I go out?"

"Go on," said Ma.

Luke glanced at his brother.

"Charley too," said Ma.

Charley squeezed his mother's hand, kissed baby Josephine, and followed his brother into the pasture to watch rescue fall from the sky.

# Mischief

We're on our way to Johnson's Pond for Independence Day, three kids, wearing swimsuits, squeezed into the backseat of the Dodge, our thighs itchy from the upholstery. Jerry, in the middle, massages his legs, pokes and pinches mine, but not Sally's. He leaves her alone because she's fourteen and big for her age and once sat on his head when he threw up on her new saddle shoes.

No matter what Jerry does, even drawing lines on my leg with a pencil, I keep my lips pressed, fighting him off with fingers. Sally ignores us, her face transparent in the window, her nose pushed against the glass like our poor dead cockapoo used to do.

Up front, our parents sit in angry silence. Even when my dad takes a wrong turn, my mother doesn't say a word. She shifts away from him and fusses with her hair, stiff with hairspray, smoothing and fluffing, fluffing and smoothing.

I don't say anything either about his mistake. Silence is safer. Besides, he'll figure it out, then spit words at my mother for not telling him sooner, slam the brakes, wrestle the sedan around the other way, threaten to go back home. I close my eyes and pretend I'm at the pond, swimming toward the raft where other kids are laughing, diving off, splashing each other.

I feel a sharp wicked pain in my side, below my ribs, and when I smack Jerry's hand away, the pencil flies up over the seat and flicks against the back of Dad's neck.

"Hey," Dad whips his head toward us.

The car jerks to the right and because we're heading up the mountain instead of along the meadow toward the pond, we crash through a guardrail and suspend in the blazing sky for one screaming moment before the ground hurtles up, bringing with it a forest of fir. Jerry smashes against me, I smash against Sally, until the windshield shatters as the Dodge punches rock.

In the first dusty moments that follow, wind stirs through the green vault around us. Sally is shaking, Jerry sobs like a baby, but not me, not yet.

# Sediment

The mind is something John doesn't want to think about. Not his, nor anyone else's, especially his wife's. Who knows what's stirring around in that head of hers these days. He watches her move from stove to sink to fridge, but what does that tell him about her thoughts, her schemes, her *soul?* For all he knows, the kitchen could be her chemistry lab, the garbage disposal her depository of failed research, and what about the freezer? Isn't that the perfect hiding place for the poisons she might someday ladle into his oatmeal?

Things weren't always like this. He used to spend time in the open, leading packs of undergrads into the mountains, mapping terrain, investigating black shale deposits, basaltic dikes, folded rock. He presses against his recliner, stares at the ceiling. This reminiscing, pondering, unbridled brain activity, none of this does any good. He needs to release that flinchy feeling of distrust and loss that quivers near his heart. Empty his skull. Find a distraction. One of those Kardashians is on the TV, showing off her ample rear. His wife used to have a rounded butt, those enticing hips, now she's skinny as a Marsh pick.

He remembers taking her to the state beach where the domes of the San Onofre Nuclear Power Station rose round and steely against a chilling sky. He hears the ocean slap at sand and rock, smells the brine, and inside the camper his fingers knead her youthful curves as if she were made of clay.

"What's going on in that nutty head of yours?" she asks, bringing him back to now.

Her damned interceptors are capable of mining every one of his thoughts. He blames those days and nights when he let her leach inside him like radiation. Don't they make alarms for this? A buzzer to give him time to wash his brain? Rid himself of her toxins? He should get out of his chair, ramble onto the deck and into the sunshine. Away from her.

He likes this cantilevered house in the foothills, its view of Devil's Gate Dam, the distant freeway, the western sun, but dusty pines groan against the railing night and day, day and –

"John, I'm talking to you."

"What?" What did he do this time? What did he say? In the past, he's accused her of affairs with the deacon at church, his cousin Dave, even the sullen grocery clerk with the checkerboard tattoo, but that was long ago. He barely talks to her now.

"You are getting on my very last nerve," she says. How he hates those thin, stretched lips of hers, but when he turns, she's gone again back to her kitchen laboratory.

The eraser in his hand feels soft, but he knows it's a figment. This happens to him now, hunched shapes dissolving into nothingness when he squints, his name called out, sharp and clear, when no one's around. He wants the Pink Pearl to be real so he can reach into his skull and rub it clean. But it isn't and he can't.

And here she is again, standing over him with a glass of something white in her hand. He frowns at the grimace on her lips. Is this *it*, the moment one of her potions will eradicate him from the crust of the earth?

But then, for a split second, she shimmers before him, the woman who once danced the Hustle with him under a disco ball, clinked glasses of champagne on a rooftop during Y2K. Hadn't they raised a Palo Alto software wizard and UC soil scientist together?

No. Not him. She'd been the one to bring them up. For the sake of science, he buried himself in the composition of the earth, its erosion, its earthquakes, its volcanic mountain building, and like his daughter, the very mud outside the door.

"John?" She holds out the glass.

He thinks: don't think. Empty your mind. Stare at the dancing light on the wall. Take your medicine.

# Cords

Shivering in yesterday's flannel shirt, no time for a jacket, I'm rushing five copies of my 613-page treatise on the Brontë sisters across town, across campus, up a gazillion stairs and into the hands of my dissertation committee when my suitcase, a two-wheeler held together with bungee cords, rolls between my car and the curb, and gets stuck. I have less than an hour to make the deadline. I tug and yank and swear until it pops free.

"Want help?"

I whirl at the voice and blink. My head riddled with No-Doz and espresso shots, I take in Aaron's ruddy face, then try to jam-jam-jam the suitcase into the open trunk, but it's caught on the spare tire that's been loose and sliding around for months.

"Kristin," he says. "Please. Let me do that."

He crowds in close, smelling of wool and bay rum, wearing the pea coat I gave him. "Scratchy" he called when he first put it on. I haven't let go of the suitcase, but now I do.

He stows it easily and closes the trunk.

I wave a hand and blurt, "Thanks, but I gotta go," then scramble into the car and start the engine. His bulky form wavers at my window, his shadow beckoning me to ask why the hell he's here, but giving in to him is all I've ever done. I stomp on the gas, the car thrusting me and my dissertation on our way.

His yowl is piercing. In my side-view mirror, Aaron stumbles on one foot, then topples to the ground.

On the way to the hospital, I tell him I've seen lots of people on YouTube get their feet run over by cars. I don't add that if it weren't for the dissertation pulsing in the trunk, the whole scenario would be funny.

He scowls. "Are you laughing at me?"

"No. Of course not. *No.*"

When I pull up to the emergency room, he wrenches himself out of my Ford, and hanging onto the door, tests his injured foot, jerks it back with a grimace.

"Wait." I bound out of the car and slip my arm around him, feel the itch of his coat on my wrist, catch a whiff of his cologne. Glimpsing his profile, I want to touch the tiny scar on his jaw, but too many years of hard work roar from the trunk.

Inside the waiting room, a woman behind the intake desk looks up, smiles.

Aaron says, "She ran over my foot."

"I didn't mean too," I blurt. "If I don't turn my dissertation in right now, I'll have to pay for another semester. That's ten grand I don't have."

The woman raises an eyebrow. "You ran over his foot."

"Not on *purpose.*"

Desperation must be dripping off me because Aaron says, "Forget it. You go. I'll be okay."

"Really?"

"Really. Go. *Go.*"

I glance back at him as I dash through the hospital door. His hand lifts in salute.

I'm on automatic pilot as I race to campus, my mind jumbled up with Aaron, the deadline, my dissertation, self-doubt. Those Brontë sisters. Were they really the rebellious, independent women I wrote about for six hundred pages? Did they pine for love? Women on the moors, their intellectual pursuits had to be much less fraught.

I'd have my Ph.D. by now if it weren't for Aaron and his wind-sailing, dirt-biking, bungee-jumping distractions. Bungee-jumping! That was the worst. Leaping from a bridge, hoping the cord wasn't too long or too worn to hold my weight, never knowing if those bungee guys actually checked everything. And the cord itself so thin, just a bunch of latex threads wrapped in neoprene or whatever it was. It was dangerous, but fun. Like Aaron.

But —

When my mother died, there was no hospital, just the morgue downtown, her Honda T-boned, the medical examiner explaining she died instantly, no suffering. Does anyone die instantly? Wasn't there terror in that split-second before? Did time slow down enough for her to deny or accept her fate? Did her life pass by like a hyper-speed movie? Did she miss saying good-bye to me? I asked myself these questions, I asked God, I asked Aaron. There was no harnessing the darkness. I clung to it. God kept silent, my father retreated, Aaron left.

A horn blares behind me. The light is green and I've somehow gotten myself to the university in one piece.


Aaron sprawls between two chairs in the hospital waiting room, his damaged foot up, his pea coat on the ground. I want to smell my armpits, but can't because he sees me as the automatic doors slide shut behind me.

"How bad is it?" I ask. There's no place for me to sit, his leg-bridge blocking the way to the couch.

He says, "Did you get your dissertation over there in time?"

"I did."

"You should look happier than you do."

"They still have to approve it." The relief – no, the *exhilaration* – I felt on my way back to the hospital is gone, but not because of any worries about approval. "How's your foot?"

"Soft tissue damage, a couple tiny bones broken. Ligaments okay."

"You in pain?"

"They gave me Tylenol."

I turn my head to stare out the window, watch an ambulance screech around the corner, its siren starting up, heading out to save the day.

I drag over a nearby chair. Perch on its edge. The glass doors glide open, bringing in a gust of cold air. I shiver, stare at my bony ankles. Wrap the cord of my purse in and out of my fingers. Wait to see where this will go.

He clears his throat. "Did you write about the Brontës?"

# Congruence

The church on the Buda side is asymmetry in stone, grinning gargoyles, gothic columns, a complex of triangulated tile roofs in terra-cotta red, aqua, white. Frosted spires prick the plane of blue sky. Inside, a thousand patchwork patterns, a quilt of painted plaster on every surface. Behind the altar, spiraling into vaults, leading upstairs to the choir loft, down into the crypt, she photographs them all.

They find a pointed arch framed with rickrack squares of rust and tan, the wall on either side arrayed with rectangles of charcoal thistles. They stand apart, yet parallel, while he waits for her to focus her camera, tell him to say "cheeseballs."

Later in the afternoon, they discover an alcove of alabaster and gilt where a stream of sun throws a sprawling miniature town into high relief, carved as tombstone above two marble bodies, man and wife, side by side. Dogs who look like lions curl at their feet. On the ceiling, angels wing.

He steps in close and takes her hand, his cool against her warmth. She leans into him. The patterns in her head come together: two horizontal beings on a slab of marble, two standing perpendicular made of flesh and blood.

# Spring Melt

Water drips from icicles outside the kitchen window. Steely skies glisten through dirty window panes. I'm pouring my first cup of coffee when I hear snow sliding down the roof and know it's time to call Carissa.

"You want me to come?" Her voice breaks a little. She's a couple years older, but I've always been the "big sister."

"No," I say. "I just felt, you know, the weight of it today."

"I feel it every day," says Carissa. "You haven't heard from Pete, have you?"

"No. He's still in jail." To change the subject, I tell her I made $250 dollars in tips last night.

"At least now, Leah, you can keep it."

After we hang up, I take a sip of cold coffee and return my mug to the numbers "1" and "3" slashed into the top of Mom's oak table. Back when snow shrouded the cabin, Pete carved the numbers – his dealer's cell – into the wood. Mom never said a word to him about it. Wouldn't, of course. Not any more. She'd forgotten how hard she'd worked to refinish the table in the first place, but I remembered. She'd been so proud of her handiwork. Then she fell in with Pete and her world narrowed down to a chunk of meth.

I run a finger over a burn in the oak, scrape crud out of the "6." Grime darkens the tips of my nails. I get up. Take a knife and washrag out of the sink. Dig at the numbers, intending to clean out the gunk, but as I work, the blade seeks to obliterate every digit.

Through the winter, Carissa and I have lived with what we've done, her down in L.A, me on the mountain. She tells me her days teaching English are filled with hypocrisy, her nights with chardonnay. I go to work at Brewster's, serving margaritas and beer, scooping pretzels into plastic bowls from bags under the bar. I shop at Vons, drop by the post office, fill my truck with gas, go to Mass, but not confession.

Now the snow is melting along the roads, polishing the asphalt, revealing discarded ski gloves, wine bottles, the occasional empty syringe. The locals emerge like bears from caves. The skiers and snow-boarders head home. I slouch down side streets dodging the cops even though they swallowed every word we fed them.

I'm late for work – Saturday lunch – me walking head down, avoiding puddles, thinking hard about leaving the mountain. Maybe I'll escape when the last of the college kids and Aussies go.

"Hey." A voice. Rough. Close to my ear. And a smell like cat pee. Pete's grip is hard. He drags me off the road, through muddy slush, and into a crowd of trees. I'm shocked at his strength. He is, after all, a middle-aged tweaker. Just like my mom.

"You got me arrested, didn't you?" He shoves me facedown into a sooty ridge of snow; digs his knee into my back. Icy crystals go into my nose. "I've been rotting in jail, waiting for trial, but guess what, the jury thought I was innocent."

I struggle against him, but he yanks off my backpack, wrenching my shoulder. Snow in my mouth. I let out a muffled scream. Then his weight lightens and I roll over. Draw in breath as he rummages through my stuff.

"Where's your money?" He jerks me up, his scabby face in mine, his eyes glittering like ice.

I cough, catch my breath. Through the pines, I glimpse the cabin. My voice comes out a strangled chirp. "Home."

Inside the cabin, Pete shakes me. "Where is it, bitch?"

"In bedroom. Chest drawers."

He throws me to the floor, my head smacking against the hardwood as he strides away to claim his booty. I curl up, wrap my arms around my ears, close my eyes. Drawers slam in the next room. Glass shatters.

I begin to scoot toward my mother's scarred oak table. Pull myself up on shaky legs, search the top for the knife.

It's not there.

Suddenly air whooshes from my lungs as he slams me to the floor again. Dollar bills – last night's tips – flutter down.

"Don't screw with me." His fingers bite into my neck. "Where's the insurance money?"

I gasp. "We didn't get –"

"Don't give me that shit. You had to. She had insurance and you killed her. I want it." His sunken eyes remind me of my mother's.

I force a soothing whisper. "It wasn't like that, Pete."

I move my leg a few inches, getting free enough to move. "She –" and I become a dervish of energy, punch my knee up and into his groin. He lets go of my throat.

I scramble under the table. The knife is on the floor. I reach out, grab for it. Can't get it. Twist closer. Get it. He's on me. My knuckles scrape his ribs. I turn my hand downward, getting the blade into the softness of his belly, and thrust up, his stench spiking my adrenaline.

The throbbing world suspends. I hold my breath. Close my eyes. See the wraith-white snow settling on the roof of my mother's car.

Pete goes still. I wait until I'm sure he's out or dead, then work my way from beneath him and crawl back under the table, folding into myself, my face wet, my nose running. And remember.

While a January blizzard pounded the cabin, my mother sat at the table across from Carissa and me, her hair the color of moldy straw, her body reduced to twigs. She picked at a scab on her lip, slid her eyes away.

"I'm a junkie," she said.

At first, we didn't understand, so she took our hands, Carissa in her left, me her right, and explained to us what she wanted us to do. Even now I can feel her bony grasp, hear her desperate "Please?"

In the end, we drove her up the mountain. Carissa fed her one last needle, we kissed her good-bye, and rolled old black Chevy into the ravine.

All winter long, it snowed like crazy, but now the snow is melting.

# Fishbowl

Mimi races up the front steps of the shotgun house, through the narrow living room, feet slapping pine, and out the back door. Auntie at the kitchen table, playing solitaire, yells after her niece, "Slow down!" but the girl's already in the Ledet's backyard.

Annie lets cigarette smoke settle in her chest, then opens her mouth, watches it swell out. Thinks of Walter. Glances at the hutch, its white paint worn to wood around the edges. A fishbowl sits on the second shelf with a yellowing photo inside of Walter, Auntie's brother, Mimi's daddy, perched on a rocking horse, taken when he was a toddler. Mimi tucked the picture in there when he went away. Said she'd take him out when he came home.

Auntie shakes herself and moves the three of diamonds onto the four of clubs. A barge sounds its horn out on the intracoastal. Giggles fly in through the open window, taking Auntie back in time, seeing herself as a kid outside with her thumb over the nozzle of the hose, humidity thick as Jell-O and Walter, dancing through the water, sliding on patchy grass, not caring about pebbles and grit scraping his chest. Mimi now, she's a firecracker just like her dad. A good thing and a bad thing.

"Auntie." Mimi at the door, pounding on the screen.

"What is it, baby?"

"Can I go down to the little store for a banana popsicle?"

"Not by yourself you can't."

"Louie Ledet's coming too."

"Is Louie Ledet paying?"

"I got a quarter. He's got his own quarter."

"Did you steal that quarter outta my purse?"

"No way. It's from my daddy. I been saving it."

"Okay then. Come right back, hear?"

"Yes ma'am," and the girl is gone.

Auntie glances at cowboy Walter in the fishbowl, wondering when he'd sent his daughter a quarter. How he'd managed to get a quarter.

Standing, she stretches. Probably shouldn't let Mimi go with Louie, just the two of them. She moves to the screen door and opens it. Bleached by the sun, the tufty summer grass stretches almost white to the canal, the water sludgy green. The bridge over Main Street is up, a shrimp boat passing through.

Mrs. Ledet is standing on her front lawn, hands on hips, glaring at Auntie. Auntie stares back. Unflustered. The woman's got to learn kids will be kids. She wasn't even here when it happened. How would she even begin to understand?

Auntie scuffs around the house, wonders what Walter's doing right now, is he thinking about Mimi at this very minute up there in that prison putting in fifteen for manslaughter? They should go see him, but it's not easy. Mimi cries for a week after they sit across the table from him, scratchy plexiglass between them, talking on the telephone as if they weren't a foot apart.

Nope. Not a fit place for Mimi, not a fit place for Walter either. Practically a kid himself.

Each fan moves hot air in circles around the house. Auntie twists up her hair and searches the hutch for a rubber band. They should be back by now. But they're too young to get into trouble, right? *That* kind of trouble? But soon she'll have to be more careful about letting them roam the

117

neighborhood. She remembers the shed at the park and its broken lock. Shivers.

Auntie slides a folding lawn chair out from behind the sofa, and sets it in the front yard, facing the sidewalk, Mrs. Ledet gone back inside. Auntie digs in her pocket for a cigarette, lights it, inhales and exhales.

There they are giggling and shoving each other, Mimi and Louie Ledet. Auntie grasps the tiny pearl around her neck given to her by Walter before he went away. Her hand sweats and the pendant pops out from between her fingers. A drop of rain lands on her nose. Nothing happens, yet everything changes.

# Broke and Broken

One hundred insipid grins from one hundred Cabbage Patch dolls mocked her. They'd emptied her bank account, invaded her house, sucked the marrow from her bones. In the maroon shadows of her darkened bedroom under the shelter of her quilt, she hides from the sly glints in their pinwheel eyes.

# Eye for an Eye

An F-150 pickup – three laughing girls crowding the front seat – knocked Jackie Dolan's mutt into heaven and kept on going. Jackie, standing the sidewalk, saw the whole thing. His grandma wasn't home so no one stopped him from stuffing his dead pet into the refrigerator for safekeeping and heading out to wreak vengeance. He knew who the driver was and he knew where she lived. He jumped on his skateboard. Took a crowbar with him.

The truck was parked two blocks over. He smashed the front windshield. He was big for thirteen and mad. The blond who'd been driving came out of the duplex with a baby on her hip, the baby giving Jackie big eyes and round lips. Jackie smashed the passenger window.

"That's my dad's pickup, you dumb-punk," the blond screamed.

"You was driving it."

"You should keep that skinny old bag-a-bones on a leash."

"You should keep that fat old baby on a leash."

"That doesn't make any sense."

"That ain't your baby. Whose baby is it?"

"Why would I tell you?" She shifted the kid to her other hip, the baby twisting around to keep eyes on Jackie.

"Maybe I wanna take that baby home to replace my dog."

"Get outta here before I call the cops."

Jackie planted his feet on the sidewalk. Held up the crowbar. "Gimme that kid."

The girl's face flickered from scorn to anger. "Screw you."

Jackie sprinted the distance between them. The girl put the baby on the grass and backed away. "I'm calling the cops. I'm calling my dad. You're gonna go to jail. You're gonna get squashed like your fucking dog." She turned and ran inside slamming the door.

Jackie glared after her, the crowbar growing heavy in his hand. He shifted his gaze to the baby who studied him back.

"You believe that witch deserted you like that?" asked Jackie.

The baby gurgled and fell on its side with a soft thump. Jackie put the crowbar down, tucked the baby under his arm, and rode his skateboard home.

Once he'd settled the baby into his own bed, Jackie said, "You know, you're gonna be happy here with me and my grandma." Jackie petted the baby's head like he used to pet Boneyard's. Scratched gently behind his ears. The baby sighed and closed his eyes. Jackie lay across the foot of the bed and sobbed himself to sleep.

A scream tumbled Jackie to the floor. The baby woke and started bawling. Jackie snatched the kid and ran into the kitchen where his grandmother was vomiting on the linoleum floor in front of the open refrigerator. The dead dog stared out from between milk and mayonnaise.

"That's just Boneyard," said Jackie. "Didn't want him to decompose."

"Hit by a car?" asked Grandma, wiping her mouth with a kitchen towel.

"Hit by a truck."

"Sorry, hon. He was a good old dog. Who's that?"

Jackie held up the baby. "This is son of Boneyard, Boneyard Junior. And I'm gonna keep him."

# Gumbo

Mom dumps two pounds of tiger shrimp into the sink. "Not done yet." She grins. I roll my eyes. Her house is heavy with the smells of my gran's Louisiana kitchen. A second pot of coffee, black as bayou water, drips in my grandpa's tiny tin pot, jambalaya simmers on the stove, and now we're making gumbo.

I have a family of my own now, thirty miles away. That's fifty bumper-to-bumper minutes in L.A, any time, but I'm making the trip more often now, trying to make it up to her, leaving my three kids with a baby-sitter, once to help clean closets, once to go through old photographs, this time to get Gran's recipes down on paper.

I start peeling shrimp while Mom pulls out the iron skillet and pours oil along the bottom. She laughs.

"What?" I ask, glad she's happy.

"Your gran always had pots going in the kitchen, then she'd scratch her head, go out on the screen porch, and yell, 'Ah, John, run to the grocery and get me some okra. I wanna make us some gumbo for lunch.' Like the etouffee and jambalaya on the stove weren't enough." She shakes her head and scoops flour into the heated oil, stirring it with a wooden spoon. "All that food and she's gotta make us some gumbo for lunch."

My mother's voice has changed to that slow-quick clip of "Sout' Lusiana." Time melts back to Dupont Street where we'd spent every summer before I left home. I can see my

122

gran sitting at her kitchen table, shelling peas, snapping beans, grating coconut. Her coconut cake appeared in every parish charity cookbook for years, but since I never liked coconut, she'd always make a small cake without it just for me.

My mother doesn't have anyone to send to the store these days, my father long gone off with a woman he'd met at church. Thinking about that now makes me angry, not for me, but for Mom. I'm all she has left, me and her grandkids, my husband too, but we're letting her down. Living on the other side of L.A.

At least she's got Stan and Kathy next door. He changes light bulbs, plunges toilets, seeds her lawn every October. Except for tennis, his boat, and his wife, he's infinitely more available to my mother than me. And I'm grateful.

"You finished peeling yet?"

I'm not, so she swirls the flour around and says, "You keep an eye on that roux." She works fast on the shrimp with a small knife to uncover the sand vein. Sweat glistens between her eyebrows. She almost looks young, blue eyes shiny, cheeks flushed. The doctors gave her a ten percent chance when they found out what forty years of smoking had done to her lungs. But she fooled them. She's still here.

The flour bubbles. When it turns to dusky amber, I throw in the chopped onions. Mom adds the shrimp. The aroma coils into memory. I breathe it in. It's heady stuff. I totter over to her desk in the corner where I dig out a piece of paper and a sharp pencil.

"What've you got there?" she asks.

"Remember, I want your recipes and Gran's. I don't want to forget —"

Bright eyes meet mine. The unspoken doesn't bother her as much as it does me. She places her hand on the back of my neck. "You'll remember."

I put my arms around her. The warm hardness of radiated muscle in her back shocks me. She's been through it all, radiation, chemo, and where have I been?

123

She pulls away and smiles. "How 'bout a quick game of gin rummy before lunch?"

We put the shrimp, okra, water, and spices on low, play cards, and talk about summers at Gran's. What it felt like to come into icy air-conditioning from the dripping sweat of outdoors to find the icebox filled with orange Nehi and Coca Cola, to hear the shuffle of cards in the afternoon, each year something different, Liverpool rummy, canasta, even Pokeeno. I can't remember how to play any of them anymore.

We eat lunch. The French bread I brought from the market is the only disappointment. When I mention this, my mother says, "Nothing like the bread we used to smell from Theriot's bakery every morning."

"I loved that, but I worried about the aroma passing over the cemetery before it got to me."

Mom smiled. "And I always thought the people buried there must've died happy because they knew they'd smell that bread for eternity."

I look up, but she's busy rearranging the cards in her hand.

At two o'clock, I kiss her good-bye, and she slips me a fifty-dollar bill. I hand it back and take plastic containers of gumbo and jambalaya instead. She watches me from her front porch until I drive safely around the corner.

The family mausoleum has been on Main Street for over a hundred years. Both my gran and grandpa are here, along with aunts, uncles, cousins, each one of them remembered in etched stone. And of course, because this is delta country, no one's underground.

The early morning sun glints in the east above black oaks. I reach out and run fingers along the smooth, cool granite. Caress the newly carved letters of my mother's name, then close my eyes and let the sweet aroma of baking French bread curl around me.

124

# The Real War

It didn't matter if it was 106 degrees or 38. We retreated as often as we could to the patch of green gravel between the asphalt street and our front porch. Ma puffed on her Newport, resting her elbow in her left fist, facing the road, her narrow back to the house.

"He slept most of the morning," she said.

"That's good, isn't it?" My father's liver cancer had cancelled out the few social skills he'd once had.

She pulled a thin blue envelope from her housecoat pocket. "You got something from your boyfriend."

"He's not my boyfriend." I took the letter from her, folded it in half. I'd "met" Frank through an ad for pen pals in a movie magazine: "Write to those brave boys serving in Viet Nam." My friends told me I shouldn't do it because we were against the war, but I didn't care. It wasn't Frank's fault he was drafted.

Ma dropped her cig onto the blacktop, smashed it with her slipper, the soles so worn I worried about scorched toes. "There's nothing wrong with junior college, honey."

How fast we always got back to this. According to her, college was a dangerous place: hippies smoking dope, dropping acid, protesting Viet Nam. I didn't answer. Instead I poked fingers against the needles of our big Saguaro cactus. I liked to see how far I could push against the spines before I saw blood.

I sent a letter to Frank once a week, each inky word sinking into the airmail onion-skin as if it were etched, giving him my life the way I wished it was, my family living in a rambling hacienda high in the San Jacinto foothills with a view of the desert, not down on the floor in a flat ugly house on Manzanita Street in a post-World War II tract. To Frank, I was going to college, too, some place by the ocean.

He sent me pictures of himself and his buddies passing joints in front of their tent, dog tags on bare hard chests. He wrote about how sick he was of humidity and rain that never stopped, the elephant grass, the smell of rot. I sent snapshots of me in a bikini and told him about the warm dry winds that swept across the desert. I left out the part about how those same winds stung the skin, sucked moisture out of eye sockets.

My parents met during the real war. He was in the Pacific; she worked for the USO. They barely knew each other when they married. When I told my mother how romantic that must've been, she crushed my hands in hers and turned away.

"I'm not bitter," she told me more than once that winter. "I seem bitter, but I'm not." She'd pat the sofa and say, "Sit and watch this movie with me." Sometimes I did, but most of the time, I was too busy finishing up school, waiting to find out which college would take me. I could almost smell the ocean salt.

In early April, when the desert sky is its crispest blue, another kind of letter arrived, but this time my mother didn't meet me outside when I got home. She'd propped it against the toaster in the kitchen, UCLA emblazoned in the upper left-hand corner.

My heart pounded as I ripped it open and read the words that would allow me to escape.

"Ma!" I shouted. "Ma!"

The house was lost in afternoon shadow, the door to my parents' room closed. I stood in the hallway, shivering in the

126

air-conditioning, listening for their usual bickering. Silence. Maybe they weren't there; maybe she'd rushed him to the hospital.

A cough from behind their bedroom door got me moving. I knocked.

"Yeah," he said.

He lay on the double bed, covers kicked off, alone in the room. His face was crisscrossed with pillow marks, his forehead creased in hard white lines.

"Sorry, I didn't mean to wake you. I thought Ma was in here."

"What's that in your hand?"

I held up the envelope. "I got accepted to UCLA!"

"Oh." He shifted his face away from me. "Get me some water."

Even flat on his back, he had the power to knock me down.

In the kitchen, I put the UCLA packet on the counter, got a glass, held it under the tap. Out the window, I glimpsed Ma's Ford Galaxie parked in the carport as it almost always was. Where was she? Had she gone to the neighbor's? But why? She'd know I was due home from school. Didn't she want to be here when I got my news? The only answer was the murmur of the air-conditioner.

"Hey, bring me that water."

I set the glass on the cluttered nightstand and helped him into a sitting position, his hot, soft skin causing my stomach to churn. He watched me do all this, his mouth a thin fussy line. I handed him the water and shifted my eyes to the closet.

One of the sliders was open, the dark recess empty. Empty? My brain took its time to catch up to my eyes.

"See?" he said. "I'm not the only one she doesn't give a shit about."

*

I never answered the letter from UCLA, didn't bother to register for junior college. After graduation, I worked at Leelie's Drugs, ringing up aspirin, flip-flops, and Revlon lipstick before going home to cook my father's dinners, keep his pills in order, change his diapers. I chauffeured him to the doctor's on my days off in Ma's Galaxie, read *Ladies' Home Journal* in the waiting room.

I continued to write to Frank about quiet afternoons spent with Ma watching TV, the beauty of the desert at sunset, the place UCLA was holding for me when I could finally go, still writing my life as fiction.

Alone at night in the living room, my father snoring down the hall, I fell into Frank's war, reading and rereading each letter, wrapping myself in their crackling blue tissue paper, their glue barely holding me together.

# Running the Fence

Davy gave the girl a shove. "Are you still Friendless-Brendless?"

She held her ground, hands on hips, knees locked, her roller skates digging into the grass.

Davy, Glen, and Glen's twin sister, Brenda, met every morning at the corner, the kids of Crescent Drive.

Glen said, "Who's she gonna play with – stuck-up Janet Box?"

Davy shrugged, jumped on his skateboard and giving a Comanche yelp, took off. Glen threw down his board, headed after him. Brenda followed, skating as fast as she could. They were eleven, it was summer, 1960, and all anyone could talk about was launching monkeys and dogs into space.

First stop was The Big "T" where the trio stocked up on candy and gum, some paid for, some not. They tapped on goldfish tanks and played hide and seek in the aisles until the lady in the wig chased the boys into the parking lot, Brenda still inside.

"Let's ditch her," said Davy. They grabbed their boards and Glen snagged Brenda's skates. They bumped over curbs, rumbled down streets, sweat stinging their eyes.

They were hunting for Delaware Punch in the fridge at Davy's house when Brenda showed up, hot and red-faced. "You stole my skates, Davy Turner."

"Send me to jail, why don't you?" he said.

"You better be careful or you're gonna be sorry."

"Cut it out, Bren. Your skates are on the front porch. Here." Glen shoved a box of Crackerjacks at her.

In the living room, they sprawled on the shag carpet watching *I Love Lucy*.

"Nothing but reruns and game shows," said Davy.

"It's too hot in here," said Glen.

Davy leaned his head back, his arm stretched up high, and poured his drink into his mouth, grapy liquid splattering down the front of his t-shirt and onto the rug.

"You're spilling all over," Brenda squealed. She ran to the kitchen, came back with a towel, handed it to Davy.

Davy tossed the towel aside. "Let's run the fence."

Glen said, "Let's run the fence."

"We're not allowed," from Brenda.

"Mom'll never know unless you tell her."

"She's just chicken!" said Davy.

"I am not." She stomped her foot.

Davy flicked his eyes in her direction. She glared at him, cheeks pink. He'd never before noticed how thick her eyelashes were.

Brenda turned and raced through the house, calling out, "What're you two waiting for?" The kitchen door slammed.

They scrambled up the chain link that separated their housing tract from the muddy celery field beyond. Eight feet of galvanized fencing rose on both sides of the cement water channel that kept the area from flooding. More chain link lay across the top, secured by heavy wire. This is where they stood, the waterway beneath their feet, a 360 view of the nearby sump, the town's small airport, and the hill where the snooty rich kids lived. Glen asked, "You think we'll all get to fly in a rocket some day?"

"No way," said Davy. "My pop says that space stuff is all smoke and mirrors, whatever that means."

Then he turned and ran along the top of the fence, and the other two followed, the metal below their feet sagging

130

and chinking in-between the cross-poles, one after the other, back and forth, three blocks one way and four blocks the other, arms spread wide like wings, until they were drunk with it and flopped, hot and sweaty, on the channel's chain link roof, the sun beating down.

They lay in opposite directions, Davy's feet to Brenda's feet, with Glen slightly apart from them sitting up, staring at a landing plane. Davy felt something push against his sneaker and looking down along the sides of their bodies, saw Brenda grinning at him. He pushed back. She did it again. He kind of liked it.

Glen groaned. "It's hot up here."

Davy said, "Let's swim in the sump."

Brenda said, "Mom'll have a cow."

"You promised you wouldn't tell." Glen stood up.

"Did not." Pulling herself to her knees, she glanced from Glen back to Davy. Bit her lip. Davy felt a little dazed. This time when he said, "You chicken?" his voice was soft.

They crawled down the fence, on the opposite side of their housing tract, and trudged through the muddy field to the sump, Davy picking up clots of muddy dirt and tossing them gently at Brenda. She returned fire.

At the sump, they took hold of this older, more rusted chain link and stared at the pit's soft asphalt sides leading steeply down into the dark water.

Brenda frowned. "I'm not going to swim in that."

"Come on. We won't swim. Just get our feet wet," said Davy.

Climbing was easy, getting through the barbed wire, painful. Their legs and arms were scratched and bleeding by the time they dropped onto the slope of the sump. The stench from the water made their eyes sting.

Grinning, Glen took the lead, leaning back as he descended to make up for the sharp slant. The tarred surface was steaming. Davy bent down to touch it, curious to see just how hot it was. Behind him, Brenda shouted, "Glen!"

Davy looked up in time to see Glen skittering down, tumbling forward, hitting his head against the blacktop, then rolling into the water.

They gaped at the spot where Glen went in. Then Brenda lurched forward, started to slip, but Davy caught her. She tried to pull away, but he held her fast, and barked, "Go get help."

"Where is he?"

"He'll come up in a second. Go on. Hurry."

She turned up the incline, then back to face Davy. Their eyes met. "Save him."

The boy nodded, then tromped down to the water. It was dirty and dark and murky, the surface rippling slightly. He waded in up to his knees. Glen should've come up by now. He glanced behind him. Brenda was topping the fence. He went in deeper, arms out, splashing and shouting "Glen!"

A sudden change in the angle of the asphalt tumbled Davy into the water. He went under. Surprise opened his mouth and eyes, filling each with gritty liquid. He couldn't see and he couldn't breathe and he couldn't find the slope under his feet. He twisted around and kicked again, groping for a sense of which way was up. His hand scraped rough asphalt and he crawled along until the sun blazed in his face. He pulled himself out, wheezed and coughed and sneezed, afraid to open his eyes. In the distance, he heard the shouts of men, the rattle of chain link. Only then did he think again about Glen.


Women hid behind hat brims and mantillas. Men straightened bow ties while crescents of sweat grew under their arms. The priest bowed his head. The moon hung like an opal in the late afternoon sky.

The coffin was as shiny as a rocket, but seemed too small to hold Glen and his skateboard, just big enough to launch a monkey to the center of the earth. Davy stood next to his mother on one side of the narrow grave. He was relieved he didn't have to see Glen inside that tiny airless box. He dropped his head. Let his tears come. His mother placed a hand on the crook of his arm.

Davy thought of Brenda, and glanced up. On the other side of the coffin, next to her mother and father, the girl chewed her lip. She looked older, thinner, paler than when they'd run the fence only a few days before. She was different now and so was he.

He willed her to look at him, to stare him down, glare at him, accuse him, forgive him, please, for not saving her brother, but she never once lifted her eyes in his direction.

# Isla Vista, 1970

It was late, the auditorium parking lot empty except for the judges standing in the shadows by the Master of Ceremonies' Cadillac, laughing loudly, and ogling pageant contestants as they retreated across the asphalt through pools of lamplight.

Lainie dropped into her Volkswagen. She was grinning. "Those dirty old men."

Karen slid into the bucket seat next to her and retrieved a bottle of champagne from the floor, began twisting off the wire.

"Open that bottle outside, will you?" asked Lainie.

Karen rolled down the window. Stuck the bottle out and popped the cork. "I can't believe you won! That story about chasing the peas around with your fork won it for you. And because you're a fascist like the rest of them." Liquid dripped over her hand as she handed it to Lainie.

"Oh stop. I'm as liberal as you are.

"No you're not, sorority girl."

Lainie took a long swig, wiped her mouth, handed the champagne back. "I never told that pea story before. Who knew I could be funny."

"You even had me in stitches. But those questions they asked you, damn, they're so lame. Wouldn't you think they'd ask about what's going on in the world? Get with the times?"

"Those people don't give a shit about Bill Allen's firing, the demonstrations, people's rights, or anything else that has to do with us."

Lainie started the car and drove out of the lot. Neither girl noticed the judges watching them leave.

"That's exactly why I don't get why you did this. You act like you don't care about what matters, but you do," said Karen.

Lainie shrugged. They had been freshman room-mates and they were still close. She flipped the radio on full blast and started singing along to "Dancing in the Street," Karen joining her, the windows of the VW rolled down, salt breeze cooling their faces.

When she saw the flashing lights just outside of Isla Vista, the angled sheriff's car, and the sawhorse roadblock up ahead, Lainie slowed and edged to the side of the road. Karen tossed the nearly empty champagne bottle into the bushes. They sat up straighter in their seats.

"Cops – assholes," muttered Karen.

The county sheriff's deputy dipped his head down to the window, the beam of his flash light picking out the face of each girl, lingering on Lainie's, the tiara still tangled in her hair.

"Turn that noise off." His voice was gruff.

Lainie shut down the radio. The usual party racket, the laughter, music, car horns, the hum of Isla Vista at night seemed different. More distant, muffled. Far off, a dog barked, followed by a couple shouts, and then a car horn.

"Would you step out of the car, please? Bring your IDs."

The girls exchanged glances and did as they were told. The other deputy moved to the passenger side and reached for Karen's elbow. She yanked her arm away and hurried around the car to stand next to Lainie.

"Have you been drinking?" the first deputy asked as he snatched their licenses.

135

Lainie stiffened. "No sir. I – we came from the Miss Santa Barbara contest."

He studied her from tiara to high heels. "Really?" He didn't sound impressed.

She looked down at the white and gold sash cutting across her blue strapless gown. "I won."

Karen let out an exasperated sigh. "Do we look like we're out here protesting?"

"Have you been smoking marijuana?" the deputy asked.

"Miss Santa Barbara doesn't smoke marijuana."

Lainie hissed at Karen, "Stop it," then turned to the deputy. "I had to be there – at the pageant – early, and I guess I forgot we might have trouble getting back in. I'm sorry. We live just a couple of blocks that way." She waved toward the barricade.

"Wait here." The deputy signaled his partner and they walked to their sedan. The girls swayed toward each other. When Karen mouthed the word "pigs," Lainie glared at her. She was cold and tired and her feet hurt.

Coming back, the deputy handed the licenses to his partner and pointed at Lainie. "You. Stand in the headlights of your vehicle."

She did it. She wasn't drunk. She could pass the test. All she wanted was to get back in the car and go home.

The deputy positioned himself in front of the car, just out of the beams. Took his time before he spoke. "Stand straight. Hold your arms out from your sides, parallel to the ground."

Lainie did this.

"Bring your left index finger to your nose."

Lainie did this.

"Walk toward me one foot in front of the other."

Lainie did this.

"Keep coming."

When she finally reached the deputy, he was out of the line of the headlights. He stepped close to her. She flinched, but his right hand gripped her shoulder.

"So Miss Santa Barbara, you've been drinking." His voice was low and rough.

She tensed up, still thinking, one swallow of champagne, nothing can happen here.

"But —" he murmured as he slid his hand inside the front of her dress. His fingers were callused and hard against her skin as he stroked her breast, pinched her nipple hard.

Feeling her nose clog, eyes brimming, she thought, he isn't doing anything to me. I'm not really here.

His breath was hot in her ear. "Keep your fucking mouth shut." He pinched her again, then his hand slithered out and he stepped away, hollering to his partner. "She's okay to drive."

Lainie stumbled back to the car, Karen already inside. The deputy's bulk darkened the window. Both girls jumped. He handed them their IDs, gave them a cheerful "Drive safe," and smacked the roof of the Volkswagen.

Once Lainie managed to get the car into second, Karen asked, "What did he say to you over there in the dark?"

Lainie blinked, her face hot. Struggled to keep her voice even. "Don't drink and drive."

"Really? That's it?"

The Volkswagen jerked and stalled. Lainie shifted back into first, restarted the engine. As the car jolted forward, she said, voice barely audible, "You're right, you know. Cops are pigs."

Miss Santa Barbara. Miss Piece-of-Shit. She pushed the nausea down, focused on getting past the barricades.

Embarcadero del Norte was lit by apartment windows, street lamps; cars moved slowly toward the Loop; one or two raced past the Volkswagen the other way. Students in groups stood on lawns drinking beer. Somewhere ahead, Lainie spotted a column of smoke. "Now what?"

"Something's burning, but I can't tell what. Let's park and go see." Karen was already reaching into the backseat for a sweatshirt.

"You can walk back, but I'm going home."

Lainie started the left turn onto her street when sirens blared, lights blinked, speeding toward them. She didn't know whether to keep going or to stop. "Can I make it?" flickered through her head just as her foot came off the gas and clutch and the VW stalled. Two deputy sheriff vehicles whizzed by heading out of town, one of them almost clipping the Volkswagen.

Karen screamed out the window, "Pigs!"

Another cop car swung around them and the girls bailed out, racing to the sidewalk.

Lainie watched a couple of guys push her VW to the side of the street.

"You okay?" One of the beer-drinking guys jogged over, pulling Lainie out of the way of deputies running toward the Loop. She was breathing hard. Leaning over, she focused on a folded paper cup in the grass. Back on the sidewalk, Karen kept yelling, "Pigs! Pigs!" and Lainie wanted to shut her up before one of the uniforms decided to use his baton, but her head was spinning. She could still see the flashers of the first cop car as it sped by. She jolted upright, remembering now that she'd actually thought she might keep turning left, keep going, even if the cops smacked into them. Now she was angry. She might have killed herself and Karen too if the car's engine hadn't cut out.

Lainie could see smoke coming from a car turned on its side, flames licking out of windows. Others joined them on the brown grass, one guy talking fast, telling them about some kid who'd been run over, the cops aiming the nose of their vehicle right at him. He'd been taken away by ambulance. No one knew for certain if he survived.

A noisy mob marched from Perfect Park toward the Bank of America, pounding trashcan lids, blowing horns, shouting and chanting. Lainie tugged on Karen's arm. "Let's go."

Karen turned; her eyebrows were pulled together, her face flushed. "I'm staying."

"Okay," said Lainie, nodding toward the crowd. "Let's go see what's going on."

"Right on."

Two of the frat boys came with them. The street was sweet with the smell of marijuana, booze, and bodies. Tension ricocheted from one person to another. Sly Stone's "We are Family" wove its way through the sirens, the rumbling conversations, the shouted slogan "7-7-7-7-6, no more bureaucratic tricks."

The windows of the bank were broken, shards of glass scrunching under their feet. They stood at first on the edge of a group of onlookers, talking, arguing, some faces creased with concern. There was another group too. The ones who seemed convinced that what they were doing was right. They were the ones clapping trash lids, singing, and "Power to the people." They absorbed the bystanders, mingled among them, infecting many with their anger. The energy connected them, turned them into one.

Lainie glanced at Karen who pumped her fist high in the air. "Power! Power! Power!" Music floated around them, a flute in time with the beat of the trash lids. Lainie chanted along.

Someone shouted. Everyone turned to see plumes of smoke coming from the bank, the blaze lighting the darkness. Lainie and Karen moved close enough to see inside the bank where broken chairs, piles of papers, parts of tables made a huge bonfire. Scattered debris smoldered or burned. Some guy was trying to stamp one of the smaller flare-ups, but as the heat increased, he ran coughing out through the shattered plate glass.

139

The crowd grew quiet as flames engulfed the building. A light wind off the ocean fed the fire. Karen, her face red and perspiring, took Lainie's hand and whispered, "You don't look much like Miss Santa Barbara now."

"Huh," Lainie said as she stared into the bright orange light.

"What really happened with that deputy, Lainie?" Karen asked. "Something happened."

Lainie gave her a grim smile, then reached down and yanked off the Miss Santa Barbara sash. She let it go and a breeze tumbled it over the sidewalk toward the blaze.

# The Last Real Human Being in Hollywood

Selene's Sunset Boulevard apartment was the two-bedroom on the left, away from the traffic, hidden behind hibiscus and bougainvillea. She'd moved in years ago when she married Hal, a Foley artist who had the place soundproofed to "save his ears for work." Back then, like now, the building had been filled with wannabe actors, actresses, writers, the occasional "best boy." Industry people, one and all.

Her neighbors sought her out, especially the young women, because walking into Selene's living room was like stepping back into 1952, onto an old movie set where Katharine Hepburn might wait for the director to yell "action": chartreuse sectional, blond wood coffee table with matching cigarette box and lighter, the bold floral wallpaper.

The starlets and wannabe starlets would hover at Selene's door, taking it all in, then let their faces split with grins. She made them sit down at the dinette and turn off their cells while she poured them mugs of Folgers coffee. The whole scene appealed to their romantic sides, their creative souls.

But what they really wanted was Selene herself. They liked to watch her move around the kitchen. They liked to let the little almond cookies she served melt in their mouths. They leaned toward her as she pulled out a chair for herself, her polyester pants as crisp as a day without smog, her perfume light and woody.

Selene was not in the business, but had worked instead for The Broadway Department Store on Hollywood and Vine in the handbag department. After a small part in *I Accuse My Parents* back in the forties, she never kidded herself about being a movie star. She liked to whisper in people's ears that her real claim to fame was having once sold a wallet to Marilyn Monroe. "Eel skin. Soft as a caterpillar."

"There's something very satisfying about selling the right purse to the right woman," she told one young tenant who fretted about her grabby agent. "You, my dear, should find a handbag with some weight to it. Metal zippers, rivets too, a woven leather and chain shoulder strap, that kind of thing."

She asked them what was going on in the movie biz these days. Who was hot and who was not. They told her everything, and she listened. There was something soft and gentle in her wrinkled face, her stained porcelain skin, the bob of gray hair, that allowed them to settle against the padded seat-backs and tell her about the blown fuse on set, the blown audition, their own blown minds.

When it was her turn, Selene talked about purses and satchels, totes and messenger bags, suede v. fabric, Coach or Hobo or knock-offs. "Avoid the cheap and plastic," she said as she patted their hands. "But the most important thing about quality leather goods is what they carry inside."

"Everyone has a dream. I lived mine," is what she told each new batch of waitresses, baristas, and Westside Pavilion salesclerks waiting for their big breaks. Most of them sat up straighter at this, lips pressed together, as they envisioned themselves climbing out of limos, adorning the cover of *People*, being pitched on TMZ. They smiled indulgently at Selene, alone in her apartment with no scrapbook of movie stills, publicity shots, award acceptance speeches. They didn't believe her. Not yet.

# 200 Nights

The oaks darkened to the color of silt as evening deepened. Mud and water, marsh grass, the rich earthy scent of coffee grounds and roses tinged the air. Scattered laughter floated across the bayou while a distant radio played accordion, fiddle, and washboard. Yvonne sat on her porch, wrapped in a scarf of memory, its silken edges frayed to confetti. She touched a gnarled finger to her tongue, rested it there.

If Carl were here, they'd be sitting on the steps and he'd reach over to caress her cheek with work-hard hands, sweetened over the stainless steel sink with Lava and almond lotion. She felt him now, folded in the gloom. Tasted his salty neck. Felt his hair dust her skin. She closed her eyes and gently rocked back.

But the memory of her daughter's insistent voice slid through the warm night, murmured in her ear. "You have options."

"Go away, little girl. Leave me be." Yvonne lowered her eyes to her own rough hands. Even out here, alone at the camp, she wasn't alone. She took in a breath, let it out slowly, and tried to conjure Carl again, but the radio music had been switched off, leaving only the sound of crickets.

What had Krista said today on the phone? "Mama, come stay with us, please. You'll be closer to your grandbaby ... and the cemetery." The cemetery, Yvonne thought. As if he were really there. She wasn't ready. Not yet. Just the thought of driving into town made her weary.

She rocked until she became aware of music again, then smiled when she recognized her own raspy voice, singing an old Cajun song she'd forgotten she knew, "... *regardez donc quoi t'as fait,/Tu m'as quitte pour t'en aller ...*" He left her, yes, he did.

Later, when the moon paled the water, she pulled herself from the rocker and trudged to her solitary bed, empty now for two hundred nights.

In the morning, she sat outside to sip coffee from an old china cup. Shrimpers puttered to their nets on the bayou, sun threaded the trees, an egret barked. When she was done, she took the tin coffee pot from the kitchen and tossed the grounds over the edge of the porch where long ago, he'd planted butterfly roses in the only glint of sun on the property. Their stems were hard tangled wood, the leaves edged brown, curling in, but the blooms were still a rich orange-red, full and heavy.

Number of days now? 201. She'd call her daughter today. Maybe next week.

# Pomegranate

When I was seven I was stolen by gypsies. Not Eastern European gypsies with their spinning dances and evil eyes, but Oregon hippies. Here's how it happened. I was skating along the sidewalk in my yellow roller skates, when a woman hustled out of bushes, her sharp claws filling my mouth before I could yell. A man helped her throw me into the back of a Volkswagen bus. They were bears, huge and gruff, from a Grimm's fairy-tale. They tied my hands behind my back. The wide tape they slapped across my lips pinched. My nose ran. My body shivered.

They took off fast, the van lurching, and I crashed face down. The carpet smelled of dog and puke and sweat. My underpants were wet and my shoulders ached. I sobbed for my mama as the van shuddered along the highway until I finally fell asleep on the warm cargo floor.

My mother came to me in spidery dreams, her face wild. She reached through the long tunneled dark, her fingers so stretched I could see muscle beneath her pale skin. But I had no arms, no way to meet her half way. My own strangled scream jarred me awake.

The VW stopped. I struggled to my knees, thinking it was over, my mama would swing open the cargo doors and fold me in her arms. Three doors slammed, but I stayed in the dark.

The man and the woman whispered as they filled the gas tank. I heard the voice of a boy. I wanted to see him. Maybe he'd been kidnapped too, but it was the man, all hairy and crusty, who cracked the back door.

"You yell, I'll hurt you," he said. "You understand me, little girl?"

I nodded and he took my thin arm in his rough hand and squeezed. I tried to twist away, but he held me fast.

"You understand me?"

I nodded again. With his other hand, he ripped the tape from my mouth and shoved in a hot dog. The mustard burned my torn lips and I bit my tongue, tasted blood, but I chewed fast, swallowed it all. He forced red juice down my throat. I choked and coughed on its bitter taste. Through a blur of tears, I saw the boy, a little older than me, pumping gas, dressed in tattered jeans and T-shirt, shifting from one foot to the other, watching. I longed for my mama.

The van rumbled through the night and another day until we reached a place between two steep walls of evergreens. The man hauled me out onto moist dirt. I smelled the ocean. Saw the boy, his back turned toward me.

My first days in the camp were spent in a hut. The floor was soft like the ground outside, and I slept on a doubled wool blanket with a shredded quilt for warmth. A window slit revealed gray sky and chilling rain. The raggedy boy delivered my food, his glare keeping me huddled in the corner until the door was locked behind him.

My only companions were vicious fleas and the ghost of my mother as I drowsed. She came to me wearing my yellow skates, circling me the same way I used to circle her in the driveway, round and round. Faster and faster she went as if she were a tornado filled with dust and the limbs of pines that would sweep me up like Dorothy and take me home. No place like home. No place like home.

The mother who flew around me in my dreams wasn't the same person who sat in our living room busy with other people's payrolls. She wore the same black yoga pants, the same oversized sweatshirt, but now her clothing was threaded with warm light, like sun filtered through a straw hat. And while her eyes beckoned me to follow her, she was alert to danger, her jaw clenched, ready for battle.

This dream mother who found me in the hut was an Amazon, Xena, a Joan of Arc. She gathered me up and crashed through the bolted door as if it didn't exist. She brought me into clear blue daylight, the wheels of her skates gliding over dirt and rocks as if the narrow valley had become a long alley of smooth concrete. I always woke up just when my mother's arms gripped me the tightest and the trees began to melt into my street, my old familiar house a half a block away.

My mother was inside that house when the bears snatched me, her hands playing the computer keyboard with the same practiced skill she had when she played the old portable organ tucked in the corner.

Was she thinking about me at all? Wondering if I'd skinned my knee on the sidewalk? Deciding if I'd like fish sticks for dinner?

How long before she slid from her chair to glance out of window and thought, "Where's Peyton?"


The light was flat and bright the day the woman who'd grabbed me, led me out of the hut and into the camp for the first time. I had no idea how much time had passed, but the sleeves of my shirt were tight around the tops of my arms. I was frightened, but relieved for the change, any change, my mind in a muddle. They could have dragged me over to the fire and branded me for all the fight I had left, but they didn't.

As my eyes adjusted to the light, I realized there were more people living in the camp than I'd thought. Dressed in jeans and peasant tops, t-shirts and sandals, beards on the men, long plaits of hair on the women, they were doing chores, cooking at a fire pit, lounging in camp chairs and under trees. They studied me as I stumbled by. My head was down, but I watched them turn back, one by one, to whatever they were doing, all but the raggedy boy. He stared, his arms folded over his chest, frowning.

I'd tried to talk to him during those days I was kept locked up. He never spoke, never smiled, but he seemed to soften toward me, putting food carefully on the ground instead of throwing it, bringing an extra jug of water, and once, leaving a Hershey's miniature under the rim of my plate.

The woman – her name was Rebecca – jabbed me in the back, nudging me closer to the camp fire where she parked me on a rock near the hairy man from the van. His beard was longer.

"You remember Stan," she said and handed me a bowl and a mug of water. Stan looked me up and down and grunted.

Rebecca sat next to me. "You're one of us now. You can walk around the camp and no one will stop you, but you can't leave. You understand?"

I put the mug down, stuffed my mouth full of beans, and nodded.

"You can be happy here," she said, placing her hand gently on my arm. "You can decide to be happy." I pulled away and her mouth changed to a snarl. Stan's eyes hardened.

The raggedy boy turned his back and walked into the trees.

*

I stayed in my hut for weeks, coming out only for meals and the chores assigned to me by Rebecca. I avoided Stan who called me "little girl" with a sneer. The folks in the camp never seemed to see me, most of them adults, some with very small children. The boy no longer brought my meals to me. I ate with the others, but said nothing. They no longer seemed to care.

In my hut, I drew pictures with a stick on the dirt floor or created shadowy shapes with my arms and hands and fingers, hummed songs I remembered my mother playing on the organ. Mostly though I slept the sleep of Briar-Rose because it was then my mother came to me.

She tried to rescue me in every dream, and after a while, her warrior stance became my warrior stance. I began to venture into the camp. Did my chores with purpose, keeping eyes and ears open. Getting a feel for the woods, the roads in and out, the rhythm of activity. And I began to run away. Each time they found me and brought me back to the hut. Locked me in for months.

I had nightmares then. My mother angry at my failures, her face turning red, tears in her eyes. I would sweat and wake to find myself glazed with dirt from the floor. I began to long for a shower and the food offered at the campfire, for the smell of pine and ocean, some kind of companionship. My mother came to me less and less, not in dream, not in nightmare. I grew to accept the way things had to be.

Whenever I gathered kindling under the pines, I found the raggedy boy there too. He told me his name was Paul and once when we were stacking wood, he said he liked my grit. I didn't know what "grit" meant, but he said it in such a way

149

that I felt a certain pride, something I hadn't felt since I'd learned to skate.

I asked him if he'd been stolen too.

He stopped and considered me, a chunk of split pine in each hand.

"I don't know," he said.

"How can you not know?"

The wood made hollow thuds as he tossed it onto the pile. "Rebecca always says she's my mother, but Stan isn't my dad."

"You call her Rebecca. And she barely talks to you."

"So?"

"So —"

The image of my real mother seared through me, sitting on the edge of the tub in our turquoise bathroom when I was little, splashing in bubbles. Paul reached for my arm, but I pushed him away and ran back into my hut. Slammed the door.

He followed. Tapped. Tapped again. I stayed quiet, trying not to make a sound, trying not to cry.

Later, much later, after Rebecca and Stan felt they'd broken me enough to not run away, Paul took me to a Farmer's Market at a commune a couple of miles up the dirt road.

The crowd of people alarmed me at first, but Paul offered up summer peaches, hot corn, and beaded necklaces. He put a fat leathery red fruit in my hand.

"What is it?" I asked.

"Something to eat."

I turned it over, looking for a place to start, digging first into the dry flower at the top. Paul laughed and took it from me and walked over to an old well. He put the fruit on the lip of the well and with his jackknife, he sawed the ball in half. Inside I saw yellow pulp and dark red seeds.

"What is it?" I asked again.

"A pomegranate."

"How do you eat it?"

"Hold out your hand."

He cut one side of the fruit in half again, and with his fingers, scooped out the seeds and placed them on my open palm. As he picked the pulp from the seeds, I felt a tingle each time his fingers pressed against my skin. He must have felt it too because when I looked up, he blushed and laughed.

I put the seeds, juicy and red, into my mouth and began to chew, but the taste was bitter. I choked and spit them out.

"What?" Paul frowned.

Tears came to my eyes and I knocked the fruit out of his hand and shoved the second half into the well. Ran off in the direction of the camp.

He caught up to me, saying he was sorry, but I ignored him. We walked back together, not talking, him touching my shoulder once and me shrugging him off. I never told him that the pomegranate tasted like the juice Stan poured down my throat on the day I was taken.

At the door of my hut, Paul put his hand on my neck, his thumb on my chin and kissed me. It surprised me. The softness of his lips.

"You were meant for me, you know," he whispered.


Whenever I began to accept my fate that I could stay in the camp forever, whenever I yearned for Paul to be near, some hidden memory or forgotten sensation yanked me into my past. I would picture my mother, hollow-eyed and gray-haired on our front porch swing, hugging her skinny legs, watching the neighbor kids roller-skate up and down the block. I imagined myself in an age-enhanced photograph on a flyer like the one Paul and I'd seen at the supermarket. We'd stood shoulder to shoulder staring at it, each of us searching for ourselves in the black and white faces. I saw Paul offering me the pomegranate, his smile vanishing as I spit out the seeds. And then the pleasant taste of his kiss.

I was happy and I was unhappy. I remembered what Rebecca had said, that I could choose to be happy. But sometimes, after these flashes, I'd catch myself at the edge of the camp staring down the empty road.

Then one morning Paul came to my hut and said we were to be together as man and wife. I knew by then my mother wasn't going to come and rescue me.

We were married by Stan, a minister of the Internet School of Theology. I wore a white dress. Though it was only a cotton shift, it was fresh and new with smocking across my breasts, something a fairy-tale maiden might have worn to wander in the woods. I felt clean and pretty carrying lilies down the center of camp, holding Paul's hand. The twenty or so residents sat on chairs and logs while Stan waited in front of the community tent.

On our wedding night, after everyone had passed out from Margaritas and beer, Paul led me to his own hut, pulled me down onto his mattress. His hands fumbled under my dress and slipped off my underwear, pinching and pulling hard enough to make me cry.

The winter lasted late into April with rain coming down most days. We stayed in bed until Paul knew every crease of my body, his touch growing gentle. It was then, when my belly began to swell, my mother came back while I slept.

Her visits were different from the webby dreams of my journey north to the camp or the warrior dreams of my first months of isolation or the frightening nightmares of my failure to run away. Now the nights were filled with milky fantasies of my mother's hand against my cheek, her lips on my hair, the warm curve of her body against mine as she

152

read to me. An expectation of happiness seeped into my bones for the child that had been me and the child I now carried.

The day the FBI showed up, dawn broke dry in the east for the first time in a week. The camp stirred with the anticipation of chores completed without mud, the opportunity to hunt and hike. But long before any of our normal activities could begin, the government agents swarmed over us like angry ants and for the second time in my life, I was snatched away from the world I knew. They crashed into our hut, guns drawn, and separated Paul and I, sweeping me away while the warmth of his hand still lingered on my stomach. I was loaded into a black Suburban next to a female agent, who gripped my hand and muttered over and over, "It's going to be all right. You're going to be okay."

I didn't recognize my mother when I was taken into the conference room in Portland. Her hair was dyed a darker brown, her eyes were smudged with age, her mouth framed with lines. She didn't resemble my conjured image of her in my last months at the camp nor the mother I remembered from our time together in the little house, her at the computer or organ, me roller-skating down the driveway and onto the weedy sidewalk.

I stood at the door, my hand resting on the place on my belly where Paul's had rested that morning. She stayed in her chair, leaning forward, her legs tensed to stand, but hesitating. Six years was a long time for both of us.

Then something in me broke and I was pressing against her as if I was seven and had skinned my knees skating. Her arms wrapped around me, the Joan of Arc in my dreams, defeating those who had stolen me away.

*

I never knew exactly what happened to Rebecca and Stan, but they must have gone to prison. When I asked my mother about Paul, she'd slant her eyes away and shake her head.

I reminded her that he was as innocent as I was, a child himself. "He was kidnapped long before me."

She tried to make me feel better, promising I would see him again one of these days, someday, maybe.

Our daughter has his intense eyes, his shy manner. I wonder if he's looking for me, for her. I dream about him most nights. And I wonder how to be happy when my heart has been split in two like a pomegranate.

# Jericho Beach

They'd gotten lost on the way to the museum. When Brooke said, "Turn right at the next corner," John had sped up. When she told him "Go back. Go back," he kept going. She sat in the passenger seat, folding and unfolding the Vancouver map, incisors gnawing the inside of her mouth, the tip of her tongue searching for blood, thinking this thing with this guy wasn't going to work. After today, it was bon voyage. *Arrivederci.* So long, Slick.

Brooke sees now the map was a metaphor, the way she'd held it in her hands, bending it one way in her lap, then another, doubling it, undoubling. Like the middle school game, it was an origami crystal ball that could be opened and closed as many times as needed to come up with the perfect combination of what she wanted and what she didn't.

But back then, when John shouted "Hey look," there'd been laughter in his voice as he finally pulled over in a parking lot, his hands loosening on the steering wheel. She turned to see what he saw: light glinting off the deep water of the inlet, sun-burnished cargo ships, a beach dotted with thick logs, lounging sunbathers. And beyond all this, snow-crusted mountains, so close they took her breath away.

He pointed to the highest peak. "That must be Whistler."

She had the map; she could have checked, wanted to check, but let it go. Through the windshield, she saw a small arched bridge, leaves shimmering in the wind, teenagers

155

tossing Frisbees on a white flowered field, and something loosened inside her.

Now, years later, Brooke is here again, this time the wind hinting at snow, the sky a hard gray. She pulls her woolen scarf over her mouth and looks across Jericho Beach to the mountains, knowing that Whistler is not among the peaks.

She will do it this time, after this trip. She's more than ready. He's coiled her up again and again over the years like a mechanical toy, tightening the key until she can't wait to spring free, disappear to where maps are just maps, and origami is a crane.

She turns toward the empty field, wind stinging her eyes, blurring both the bridge and the copse of trees beyond, where he'd teased her about how easily her walls tumbled down on Jericho Beach.

A shout wheels her around. Here John comes, gripping paper cups of coffee, striding across the sand toward her, their daughter tagging along with doughnuts. Brooke waves, her fingers rippling, then folding and unfolding, remembering. As if she could have chosen then. As if she can choose now.

# Ruby

Ruby meanders through icy streets in t-shirt and ragged jeans, a dirty woolen coat loading her down, its collar made of lynx. She's never seen a lynx, yet she can conjure a field of scattered snow, clumps of brown grass bent in sunlight, and something white and feral crouched beneath the aspens.

The coat's fur used to be soft, but now is stiff, like her hair gets after grimy days outdoors or when she trips on the curb and lands in muck. She falls often enough that purple knots form below her skin so when she makes her way to the shelter, volunteers gently touch her bruises and search her skull for cracks and lice, feed her Costco lasagna, let her shower.

Perched on her favorite rock in Central Park, she watches young women in fancy boots and newly-purchased coats scurry home from work. She wonders what that feels like, cold breezes on smiling faces, welcoming arms at familiar doors.

She clambers down, but her feet slide against the rock. She hits the dirt hard, her head thudding against granite. Dizzy, she stares into the park. No one notices her. No one ever does.

Tightening her paper robe, Ruby steps out of the shower at the shelter to find Mrs. Lee waiting on the metal bench in the locker room. She likes Mrs. Lee. Still, she turns away, pretending the woman, one of the volunteers, has chosen this dank space because she likes the smell of dispenser shampoo.

"How's your head?" asks Mrs. Lee.

Ruby fiddles with the locker's sliding mechanism. There's no padlock, no lock of any kind. Someone could steal her clothes. It's happened before.

Mrs. Lee says, "I have something for you. You might remember it today."

Ruby moves her head enough to see the torn slip of paper in the woman's hand. In her mind, the girl glimpses a different locker room, a high school locker room, maybe the one in Idaho, or was it Alberta? Someone gave her a note then too. Ruby presses fingers against her chest, her breath skittering in and out.

"Doesn't this belong to you?" asks Mrs. Lee.

Ruby drags the sleeve of the paper robe across her forehead. "No."

"It has your name on it. Take a look."

The paper is dry and fragile between Ruby's fingers, its blue lines barely visible beneath the words. She hands it back, stares down at her disposable shower shoes.

"Are you sure?" Mrs. Lee frowns, but not unkindly. "Don't you want to keep it? Maybe it will help you remember."

Remember what? Ruby has the field of snow, the white lynx in the trees. Isn't that enough? "That's not me. It's not mine. Not mine." She smacks the locker with the palm of her hand, rubs her forehead again.

"Okay. It's okay." Mrs. Lee stands, starts to pat the girl's thin shoulder, but changes her mind, backs away, toward the swinging locker room door.

The slip of paper is on the metal bench. Ruby counts to 100 before she reluctantly picks it up and studies the blotchy scrawl. "Please excuse Ruby Slater from classes today as she needs to ..." The rest of the note is torn away.

She puts on the clean jeans and t-shirt Mrs. Lee has left for her. She strokes the matted fur of her coat. It was white once; she's almost certain.

She stops at Mrs. Lee's desk to return the scrap of notebook paper and says, "I don't know what this other Ruby wants. I can't help her."

"I'll save it for you," says Mrs. Lee. "Just in case."

Ruby frowns. "In case of what?"

"In case you ever want to go looking for the other half."

Ruby rubs her cheek against the collar of her coat and turning away, trudges into the night.

She stops at a corner. The light is red. She wonders, "What other half?" just as the glow of green calls out to her.

# Blusterfuck

Your best friend, Layla, thinks the fresh scent of pine needles will do you a world of good. You agree, considering your recent hassles with dividing up the furniture, the Journey albums, and the road sign collection you both spent nights in jail for and if that isn't enough, there's your teenage son's obsession with werewolves to worry about.

You stride into the living room of Layla and Henry's luxe mountain cabin, your overnighter catching on the door jam. You've driven three-hours in the clunky Subaru because your ex claimed the Caddie in the divorce.

Henry is sprawled on the couch watching a sports-talk program – something about the Dodgers – and holy crap, next to him is Rex the blow-hard, the braggart, the Blusterfuck. It's all you can do not to flip a bitch and head home. Then Henry, lovely, oblivious Henry gets up and gives you a hug. Blusterfuck grunts a greeting over his shoulder.

You met B-F before with his wife so why the hell doesn't he at least paste a grin on that tubby face of his and say, "Hey, how you doing?"

But no. Eyes glued on the TV screen, he says to Henry, "You know my dad drank beer with Koufax. I shook hands with Garvey and The Penguin."

Henry's eyes go wide. "Steve Garvey?" and you decide it's time to search for Layla and Blusterfuck's wife, old What's-Her-Name.

You don't remember much about his wife because when Blusterfuck's around, he opens his mouth and vacuums the room dry, pulling every last dust mote into his gut. Even the skin cells of your own face feel like they're going to peel right off and zoom down his gullet.

There she is, B-F's wife, standing out there on the back deck with Layla, drinking Chardonnay – or maybe it's just a shadow cast by one of the redwoods? With old What's-Her-Face, it's hard to tell.

Later, down on the dock in lawn chairs, the five of you drink cocktails and watch the sun drop behind the peaks; Blusterfuck announces he's a wine connoisseur. "One of my college buddies owns a little winery in Santa Inez." And a chef: "My aunt went to high school with Alice Waters and I gotta say, there's something to be said about organic cuisine."

In the growing dusk, What's-Her-Name, B-F's vaguely there mate, coughs. At least, that's what your under-developed echo-detection skills tell you, but B-F ignores her, too deep in his dissertation on the differences between pure olive oil, virgin olive oil, and extra virgin olive oil.

Over-grilled sirloins and iceberg lettuce wedges, Henry mentions golf. You quickly ask What's-Her-Name if she plays golf.

The woman looks startled, unaccustomed to being spoken to directly, and before she musters the ability to form words, B-F says, "Oh she'd be good if she practiced her swing. She uses too much shoulder. I try to show her …"

You glance at Layla who shrugs and you sit back against the cushion to take an eyes-open nap.

Bluster-Fuck's voice, its expansive tenor, the occasional trumpeted pronouncement, makes you cringe. He segues from golf to tennis, his tennis elbow, his new top-of-the-line-racquet – blah-blah-blah – the agonies and ecstasies of being a real estate developer, day-trader, ad-hoc advisor to the town council – blah-blah-blah – beloved husband, little league coach, adored father of three highly intelligent and successful children one of whom is dating a billionaire's granddaughter with houses in Maui, Vegas, and a co-op in New York– blah-blah-blah. He yammers about his mother whose refrigerator he's just repaired, his uncle who takes him to the Dug-out Club at Dodger Stadium, the sexy neighbor who has a crush on him. Every once in a while, you unglaze your eyes to see if his mouth is cramping, but notice instead the bobbing of his stubbly red neck, and you want to barf.

He sees himself as jovial, hilarious, but humble, too, don't you know, just another wealthy Joe out of Westwood. You, however, have a different take, and picture him head down in the toilet, under the wheels of your Subaru, or better yet, down the mountain, tied to a railroad track for the 4:30 Amtrak pass.

Dishes done, coffee brewing, the fragrant smell of baking shortcake fills the kitchen. You and What's-Her-Face are cutting up strawberries, Henry's whipping the heavy cream, Layla's digging out silverware, plates, and napkins. Blusterfuck's flapping his jaw. Of course he is. "You know, I give the produce manager at Vons tickets to the Lakers a couple of times a year and he always saves the best berries for me –"

Some switch in your brain toggles "on" and you finally raise your voice. "I saw a terrific movie the other night –"

Blusterfuck: "Me too. Oh, you shouldn't use a knife to take off the stems –"

You (a little louder): "The movie is based on an ancient Roman play –"

B-F (louder still): "We went to Rome last month. Paolo Regetti, the famous Italian historian –"

You (very loud): "The movie is about an Italian soldier who brags –"

Layla (shouting and giving me a look): "The shortcake's burning!"

B-F grabs a kitchen towel, dives at the oven, and pulls out the golden cakes. "Ta-da. These are perfect. I'm just in time to save the day!"

You give up and chop strawberries, stems and all, into the bowl, each stippled berry reminding you of Blusterfuck's jiggling neck. When the twice-sharpened knife winks at you, conjuring up the urge to slice Blusterfuck from stem to stern, you high tail it out of there, glad you haven't unpacked the weekender, and you've still got some gas. Glad too, that maybe you don't have it so bad.

# Flash Flood

Night off from the 7-Eleven, and I flick on the TV to watch a rerun of *Sharknado*. Instead there's some news guy – the geeky out-in-the-field kind of guy who gets the sideshow gig, not the behind-the-desk gig – reporting from a disaster research facility about what to do if your car gets swept away in a flash flood. With you in it.

Apparently there is a procedure to deal with this.

I live in the desert, so I don't give much thought to the possibility of me landing my hatchback nose-down in the drink. But out here among the cacti, dry creek beds can suddenly swell into raging rivers of water, sand, and debris. I prop my feet on the empty milk crate to watch.

The guy in the white coat with the plastic badge over his heart says, "In case of a flash flood, the first thing to do is open the windows and let the water in."

Are you fucking kidding me? Open the windows?

The geeky reporter lets his brows furl together. "Isn't that counter-intuitive?"

Fuck, yeah.

The researcher is fiddling with his badge, then remembers he's on camera. His head startles up. He flashes a smile. "Yes, of course, but it's essential to prepare as many exits from the vehicle as possible."

Hypothetically, I'm strapped in an automobile that weighs two-three-thousand pounds, dragging me deeper every second, and he wants me to take the time to prepare.

Let the water in, my ass.

The researcher senses my panic. He looks through the camera right at me slugging down a Kilt Lifter ale, and says, "Stay calm."

Stay calm? I finally meet a woman I can tolerate – she's in the shower right now running her hands over her Tara Reid breasts and I'm out here trying to get the 411 on how to save myself from drowning in the fucking desert? Calmness is *not* part of this equation.

Wait. On TV, the guy in the white coat is helping a woman into a cable car-looking thing suspended over a huge tank of water. What did I miss? What's the reporter saying?

"According to researchers here at the institute, in order to open the door of your vehicle under water, you will have to wait for the pressure on the inside and the outside to equalize."

Hold the fuck on! Let me get this straight.

I open the windows and sit in my beater until the water on the inside is the same amount as the water on the outside. Are these people insane? I'm plummeting into oxygen-deprived liquid and this asshole wants me to wait? WAIT?

Back to the researcher whose badge I notice is about to fall off.

"Be sure to keep your seatbelt on so you can remain in control of your movements, especially if there are small children with you."

Keep my seatbelt on. That doesn't sound right. Wouldn't I need to release the seatbelt to swim out the open window once the damn pressure is equalized? But I'm riveted. They're showing a seatbelt slicing tool with a safety edge. Is this something I can pick up in the automotive section at Wal-Mart? Where would I keep it? In the glove box?

Now the woman who climbed into the experimental cable car thing with the help of the white-coated man is up to her eyebrows in water.

"Why is she keeping her eyes closed?" asks the reporter. Good fucking question.

The man in the white coat smiles. He no longer has a badge. "Visibility is poor so it's better to deter the oil and pollution in the water from damaging your eyes by keeping them closed."

Let me recap.

In case of plunging into a river during a flash flood, I should do the following:

Hold my breath.

Stay calm.

Open all the windows and let the water in.

Keep my seatbelt on.

Keep my eyes shut.

Wait for water to fill the car.

Dig through the glove box to find the tool necessary to free my body from the seatbelt.

I switch off the TV and beg the woman with the Tara Reid boobs to climb back into bed with me. I silently pray for drought.

By the time my lovely companion slips out the trailer door, snagging the twenties I left on the counter, the pressure on the inside and the outside is just about equal.

# 6 A.M.

At the breakfast table, she shifts her chair to the left, angles her body away. He reads Plaschke in the *Times*, his hair the gray of her favorite scarf, lost now for two or three years. She remembers that scarf. How it settled comfortably on her neck, feathery soft, like breath. The sheen of it seemed enchanted, changing from gray to almost blue with the navy of her dress. Paired with her red coat, it was silver.

She glances at him again, hidden behind newsprint and wonders if she were to empty her drawers on the bed and sort through panties and bras, she might still find that rectangle of shiny wool.

She sighs, turns back to her Sudoku. More empty squares than full ones. She works the numbers, circling, filling in the obvious.

Monday puzzles, she keeps everything neat, her goal to have no extra marks in the boxes, no false starts, and nothing covered in whiteout. Tuesdays too, but it grows harder.

By Friday, she keeps her guesses tiny: miniature 2s, 3s, 4s, her 7s crossed through European style so she doesn't mix them up with 2s. Yet the sloppy whiteouts increase, the paper tears, the numbers bleed together. She swabs her glasses, tightens her teeth, and steadies her extra-fine Pilot pen while her husband pushes himself away from the table.

# Small Gifts

As a kid Bobby knew no fear. He played war games with his pals till the sky grew black. Breezed down hills on his bike, no brakes. Sprayed paint in boxy letters and numbers on walls. Stole gum and rum. His whole youth, he ranged through streets like a thug. His ma bore all his teen boy crimes, and when he swung up on a train aimed south, she wished him luck. He did not see the loss in her eyes nor did he feel the clutch of her hand on his arm. Oilrig wealth pulled him toward the Gulf.

He went from job to job, and once in a while he felt the tug of home, to go and see his ma, wed an old flame, buy a house. But he loved his lot, loved his work, and when the urge to give it up took hold, a fresh quest would thrust him on a plane to a new field, a new hole in the sea.

Bobby was "House Mouse" for a steel rig in the North Sea when his ma's heart failed. He got off work so he could lay her to rest, and since he was a rough man, a hard man, he denied the ache.

His ma was one of plain taste, so he bought a pine box, one white rose. At the church, he shook his head and let her friends tell him how proud she was of her strong bold son and when the old folks were gone, he stood for a while flanked by the graves of his ma and his pa and said a short prayer.

When he turned to leave, a priest came close. "She was a sweet soul," he said.

"Yes. Yes, she was."

"She saved you much pain, you know."

"I know." Bobby bowed his head, thought of how she'd talked the cops out of youth camp, out of jail too. He loved her for it.

The priest came close. "Did you know your pa died the day you were born?"

Bobby looked up. "That's not true. Look at his stone, the date. He died in March. I was born in June."

"That was your ma's doing. She didn't want his death to haunt the day you were born. She didn't want his loss to cost you more than his lack. It's the small things they do for us, our mothers, that we don't see, that let us be who we are. That was her gift to you." The priest patted his arm, turned, and moved down the knoll to the church.

Bobby wore no coat, no hat so the wind whipped his hair, made his cheeks burn red, and for the first time he let the tears come.

# What's Left

## 2010

She gives up knitting needles for the smaller steel that comes with buttercups stenciled on muslin and predetermined thread. No counting in embroidery. Diligence, not thinking, is required. Good light. Glasses.

She should shackle those glasses on a chain around her neck, but she favors a housecoat pocket. Now they're lost.

## 1995

She can't find the phone number she scribbled on the torn bit of newspaper. She returns to the diner where they met, but the waitress with dyed yellow hair doesn't remember him. Doesn't remember her.

She eats lettuce with Thousand Island at the counter every night until they padlock the door, tear down the building.

## 1980

Her husband calls from his Porsche to tell her about the paralegal he's knocked up. She slides down the counter to sit on the kitchen floor. Onions smoke and blacken the skillet. A mechanical voice tells her to please hang up and dial again.

# Last Four Songs

Morning light bends through leaded glass. Patterns form and reform on sky-colored walls. Frances wakes. She's dreamt of dew under bare feet, that boy with his hand on her waist: his warmth, her warmth. She breathes remembered air, crisp and meadow sweet. Rolls to her side, wraps herself in the softness of her comforter. He'll come for her again today. He's promised a maze of lacy oaks, a stroll down speckled paths, the sound of rustling grass. Around her now, beads of light dip and dart. Windchimes on the porch below beckon.

That boy. Frances moved on – she had to – but sometimes when dawn sharpens dark edges, she remembers how his fingers burned her skin. Like this morning when her daughter banged into the house and threw her purse across the family room, hitting the bookcase, knocking the Waterford vase to the floor. Crystal shards scattered across the hard wood, settled into the carpet. When her daughter shrieked, "I'm pregnant," Frances slapped her hard across the face, almost knocking her down. She should've remembered then, about that heat. That boy. Killed on his motorcycle when a truck ran a red light so many years ago.

Her husband spends time in the garden, earphones plugged in, a rake or a hose gripped in one fist, a can of Fresca in the other. He's out there most afternoons when Frances comes home from school, essays to grade tucked under her arm. He's here now, shooting water onto a rose bush, not hearing the car door slam. Frances slips into the shadow and chill of the kitchen, shrugs off her coat and tumbles her work onto the table. She flicks on the light. On the refrigerator is a picture of her granddaughter in cap and gown. She sighs and turns away to dial her iPod to Richard Strauss, pour vodka into a half-empty Fresca can, and trudge upstairs to bed.

Under California's winter sun, Jerry's rosebushes burst with bloom, 'Black Magic', 'Secret', 'Golden Celebration'. Frances, still in her robe though it's near sunset, bends to sniff a 'French Perfume'. She closes her eyes and imagines him behind her, arms wrapped around her, his mouth pressing into her hair. How he loved his garden, how he loved her. That boy – so long gone – lingers, but it is Jerry she remembers. Strong, sweet, quiet Jerry. Gone too. Soon the yardman will come to prune and leave her with a garden of sticks, but for now, in this moment, she is content.

# Saddle Shoes

Kathleen wanted a pair of saddle oxfords, real ones, not because they were cool, but because the ridge between the sole and the shoe itself would allow her to tighten the clamps of her steel roller skates securely in place. She couldn't count on her beat-up Mary Janes. Every time she'd bump over a curb, a skate would fly off and she'd find herself sprawled on the asphalt, the goose in the neighbor's yard honking and flapping wings.

Her mother said, "If I buy you oxfords, and I'm not saying I will, but if I did, you couldn't wear them to skate. That would just ruin them."

Kathleen protested. "I could get killed."

"Then don't skate in the street."

"I don't skate in the street, but I have to *cross* the street."

"No you don't."

Kathleen bit her lip.

She got saddle shoes for her birthday, but owning them wasn't the point. She'd wanted them for a reason, a practical reason. The other girls admired their shiny newness, and even Margaret Horton smiled at her, but she went back to wearing her sneakers to school. They were lighter and more comfortable, and she couldn't help but resent the black and white oxfords.

Saturday mornings, she strapped her old Mary Janes into her skates, and secured them by wrapping ties she'd cut from her mother's apron. She banged off curbs at Avenues D, C, and B, falling less often, and trundled around the school playground doing figure eights and chasing basketballs for the boys.

Her skates rusted in the back of the closet when she moved on to books. Sitting in the living room, her bare feet dangled over the arm of the loveseat. She loved Scout and Tom and Huck, wanted a dog like Buck, and soon graduated to Emma, Hester, and Jane.

During high school she lived in the library, bending over a table, her sneakers untied, looking at maps of the world or rereading Dickens. And though she went to her senior prom with a math wizard who wore basketball shoes and she wore satin pumps, Kathleen preferred to wear sandals and flip-flops and this inclination informed her life. Eventually, she packed herself off to Oahu and wrote ad copy for Liberty House, spent time at the beach watching sunsets, and got herself a dog. She named him Buck.

# The Old Road

## A Novella

A clock just struck within some house remote.

Which house? — I long to still my beating heart.

Rainer Maria Rilke

THE OLD ROAD

RIO LITO CREEK

GD

# Contents

# The Stranger

If a stranger jogs along in woolly darkness, he might wonder about this neighborhood on the edge of town with its scrub oak and sycamores sloping toward a creek on one side of the Old Road, and a mishmash of houses on the other.

A sharp night wind chills the stranger's forehead, seeps inside his running clothes. He glances up at the Spanish revival cresting a knoll at the end of a long narrow walkway. Yellow light pools along the driveway.

He slows and pivots toward a bungalow built close to the sidewalk on what might have been land belonging to the hilltop mansion, but clearly isn't, sold off and subdivided, maybe during the Depression, a hedge growing between the two.

Scaffolding criss-crosses the side of the darkened bungalow, wind raps a large pine against its gabled roof, a ladder lays abandoned on the grass, and beyond a second hedge, on the corner of Portola and the Old Road, sits a small Tudor house.

A slight curve in the road and eugenia trees dancing in the rising gale, obscure the property to the north. The stranger clears his throat and trots on slowly, shoulders hunched to his ears. After a couple dozen steps, he stops in front of a group of refurbished vacation cabins, built a hundred years ago.

These little houses surround a courtyard, two on each side, one centered in the back. A dog yaps from one of them. Light gleams here and there. Oak branches crackle as the wind blows steady. The stranger allows himself a smile.

Inside the front cottage, Jamie peers out the window, hair clipped back from her neck, the yellow glow behind turning her to silhouette. It's too dark for the stranger to see the crease between her brows, the grim set of her mouth, but what tells him everything, is the wilt of her shoulders.

When she retreats from the window, he turns into an unyielding wind, trotting back to his car.

# The Storm

Jamie turns back to the living room where Lily and Collin stretch out across the floor watching *The Neverending Story*. Joel brought the VCR back from one of his trips, "Property of Lincoln Motel" scratched on the back. What will he bring home this time? Ice bucket? Shower curtain? Those little soaps and shampoos and cellophane-wrapped candies that make the kids squeal when he empties his pockets?

"I'm hungry," says Lily from her spot on the carpet.

"Okay," but before Jamie heads into the kitchen, she peeks through the curtain again. A whoosh of wind rattles the glass; a door slams; across the courtyard at Mr. German's, a light snuffs out.

"Mom." Impatience from Lily. "Hungry."

Jamie reaches into the freezer for Costco pasta, and while she waits for the water to boil, she punches in Joel's phone number. When his voicemail greets her, she jabs the disconnect icon and skids her cell across the countertop. He said he'd be home tonight, but maybe not tonight, "maybe" meaning for them to go to bed and not to count on him. Ever. She scissors open the ravioli, nips the tip of her finger. Yelps. Another gust jangles outside of the cottage. Lily appears in the doorway, feet apart, hands on hips, eyes wide. Collin pushes around her and hugs his mother's legs.

After baths and stories, Jamie picks up the syllabus for her new class. School's just starting, but what's the use, community college, taking one class a semester, when she doesn't even know what she wants to do?

She returns to the window. The moon hangs bright, the sky, wind-scrubbed. Tattered leaves twist and scuttle down the Old Road.

Glimpses her cell. Still nothing from Joel. Damn him. She's sick of it.

Jamie quietly slides open drawers in the kids' room, pulls out underwear, t-shirts, jeans, sweatshirts.

A groggy "Mom?" comes from Lily's bed.

Jamie whispers, "Time to sleep, honey."

In her own room, Jamie dumps the clothes on the bed and realizes she's forgotten their shoes. She'll get them in the morning, she decides, as she drags the big blue Samsonite from the closet. Better not risk waking Lily again.

She's asleep when a thundering crack, a ferocious shudder, sends her hurtling from the bed. Earthquake! The kids are screaming in their room.

She hollers, "Get on the floor by the dresser! Scrunch down! I'm coming!" as she flies into the living room and crashes headfirst into something that shouldn't be here, something sharp scraping her face, something sharper stabbing her ribs. The smell of dust and dirt fill her nose.

Then, the house isn't shaking any more. Cold air sweeps through her, and looking up, beyond the giant branches of a tree – a *tree?* – she sees a spray of stars. How did the night sky get inside her house?

She blinks. It's the oak. Crashed through the roof. Onto her living room floor.

Jamie struggles to stand, her sweatpants are caught on a broken branch. She grabs at the cloth and yanks and yanks, panic clogging her throat.

"Mama!" from Collin.

"We can't get out!" from Lily.

"I'm coming." Scratching, thrashing, cursing, Jamie drags off her pants and tries to climb into the living room, but a limb cracks under her weight and she tumbles forward, her knee smacking the ground. Hard. And where the hell is Joel? The asshole.

She battles out of the snarl of wood and prickly leaves, crawls back into her bedroom for Joel's baseball bat, smashes her bedroom window. She knocks away shards, scrambles onto the dresser, and leaps into the chill. Wind stings her legs, waters her eyes. A man rounds the corner of the cabin. Joel! But it's not him. Someone built like him, but older, heavier. Stumbling to her feet, Jamie shoves the man toward the window of the second bedroom. Hands him the bat. "My kids! Help me get them out."

# Neighbors

Lit by candles and a kerosene lamp, the tenants crowd the landlady's living room like flickering ghosts. The man, the one who helped rescue the kids, clears a space on the wicker sofa for Jamie, then hands her a blanket to cover her legs. She lets the children settle on her lap, wincing from her cuts and scratches, feeling out of body, out of time. Gusts howl at the edges of the cottage.

Her voice breaks as she says, "Thanks for helping me get them out."

"Glad I was there. How old are they?"

"Three and five."

"Nice kids."

"They are. You a friend of Sybil's?"

"Not really." He scans the crowded room. "See that old man over there? The one fussing with the mutt?"

"Gus? He lives across from us. I'm number 1, he's number 2."

"He's my dad."

"I didn't know Gus had a son." She squints up at the man, searching for similarities, maybe the nose, the chin.

"I'm not surprised," he says. "Name's Mars. And you are?"

"Jamie Prentiss." She glances at Gus, curious about him and his son, but too drained to engage, she changes the subject. "How bad is it outside? I can still hear it shrieking."

"Wind up to 90 miles an hour." Sybil glides over, wrapped in one of her Hawaiian print robes, bringing a tray of instant coffees. Mars takes one, nods at both women, and wanders away.

Sybil passes a cup to Jamie. "I guess you couldn't wait for me to put a skylight in your cabin. Glad you're all right. Your husband's not home, I take it?"

"No, he's roofing in Fresno."

"A roofer who no longer has a roof! You have your phone, honey?"

Jamie shakes her head. The landlady hands her a cell. "Use mine. How about some hot chocolate for the kids? Might as well drink the milk before it spoils. The stove's gas, but we may not have electric for hours."

"Thank you. They'd like that." She watches Sybil thread her way through the clutch of neighbors. Tall and lean, Ian Shane bends over Mrs. Renke sitting in a rocking chair while Gus stares out the window, his little dog shivering in his arms. Mars follows Sybil into the kitchen.

With an exhausted sigh, Jamie taps numbers, splutters into the cell, "Come home, Joel. A tree killed our house." She starts to disconnect, then puts the phone to her mouth again. "Or *don't*."


After Lily and Collin fall asleep on their mother's lap, Mars carries them one at a time into Sybil's second bedroom while Jamie ducks into the bathroom to put on a pair of the landlady's silk pajama bottoms.

She meets him in the tiny hall. "Thanks again, Mars."

"Not a problem." His eyes hold hers for the briefest of moments – warm and sympathetic – before he turns away into the living room.

As the storm quiets, the sun creeps up, revealing a ravaged neighborhood littered with broken limbs, uprooted trees, piles of leaves. An electric pole is splintered in half, its wires strewn about, the corner stop sign bent at 45 degrees. Sirens in the distance announce apocalypse. Sybil's tenants as well as the young couple from the bungalow next door and the old couple from the Tudor gather along the sidewalk, muttering about the mess, the noise, and the miracle that no one's seriously hurt.

Jamie gawks at the giant horizontal oak, the house sheared down the middle: chaos and debris on one side, what's left of her life on the other. Light sifts through branches, dust motes hang on air, her suitcase, the Samsonite, barely visible, lays squashed under the foliage.

Mars slips up, startling her. "Not so good morning, huh?"

She shakes her head and picks her way around the ruined cottage to her bedroom window.

Mars ambles behind. "Kids sleeping?"

"Sybil's feeding them Cheerios. I need my phone. Joel probably left me a message."

"I can climb in and get it for you."

"Thanks, but just give me a boost. I want to look around."

"So your husband hasn't come home?" he asks as he bends over to offer his clasped hands as a stepstool.

Jamie doesn't answer as she crawls through the empty window frame, careful of residual glass, and onto the dresser. She slides to the floor and searches the bedroom for her cell.

Mars peers in. "I can help you clean up if you want."

"Thanks, but I can't think about that right now."

"Too soon. I get it. Find your phone?"

"Yeah." She holds it up, moving toward the living room door, but can't get through because of the oak.

"Any messages?"

"Yes," she lies and angles away from him.

# Empty Nest

Sybil's on her porch in the silk robe she ordered from the Internet, just warm enough for a California morning. She sips sugared coffee and studies her bunions, swollen ankles, the varicose veins tracing up her calves, all the while keeping an ear out for the blue jay. She's filled the crystal candy bowl on the table next to her with sunflower seeds, a peanut or two. It's been a month since wind roared through the Old Road at 90 mph, knocking down trees, severing electrical wires, turning the neighborhood into a disaster area, a month since Louise Renke's heart attack put the old lady into a nursing home, a month since Jamie and the kids climbed into their dilapidated Honda Civic and disappeared, a month since Sybil last saw the jay.

Her bones ache, but she closes her eyes, listens to the sound of leaves, and remembers tromping down to the creek as a kid, the blissful freedom of it all, she and her cousin Dale exiled to Grandpa's for the summer, sleeping in twin beds in the spare room when they were young, fishing early on dewy mornings, and later when they were teens, doing other things in the tall brown grass after Grandpa made Dale sleep on the living room sofa.

Most of her property has been cleaned up by Gus German's son, Mars, and a couple $10 street corner laborers with rakes and wheelbarrows, but the front cottage where Jamie lives – lived – with her husband and two kids is still buried beneath the fat trunk and broken branches of the two-hundred-year-old oak, red-tagged by the town as uninhabitable. As for the blue jay, with his smart-aleck chirp and curious nature, he too lost his nest when the giant tree crashed down.

"Morning, beautiful," Ian Shane calls from the porch of cottage number 4.

Sybil keeps her eyes closed.

"I know you're awake." He's the newest resident in Sybil's domain, a thirty-two-year-old man whose mother, Rita Shane, a real estate agent, employs him to sit on her open houses, help "stage and polish" her listings, flirt with female clients. She also pays his rent, one of the many parental trends that cause Sybil to wonder what the world is coming to.

"You're up early," she says. "Want some coffee?"

He strides over on long legs, his lanky body awkward in a dark blue suit, light blue shirt, pink tie, his eyes cobalt, his grin charming. "Love some. Any word from your insurance company yet?"

Sybil grabs a paper napkin and dusts off the other rattan chair. "They're taking care of it, though I haven't seen any money yet."

"There's an emergency loan center over at City Hall to help with storm damage. If you dress in that hot yellow dress of yours, they'll whip out their check books."

"I've owned this place free and clear for forty years, Ian Shane, and I'm not about to go into debt now. Let me get you that coffee." She disappears inside, thinking, she never did learn to keep her distance, even though Grandpa warned her to stay away from the paying guests.

Probably Ian's blue suit. She's missing the jay. That's it. However, talking to the bird is a lot more fun than talking to Rita Shane's son.

She returns from the kitchen with a small thermal pot, another cup, and a plate of chocolate biscotti on a tray, and the man's face lights up.

"You know, Sybil, you're sitting on a gold mine."

"I've got a shovel if you wanna start digging."

He laughs a bit too loud. "I'm serious. Don't you want to be done with this headache?"

"There's always some headache, Ian. Don't you know that yet? You want Splenda or real sugar?"

"But you don't have to deal with this one." He nibbles on his biscotti. "Have you been up to the new restaurant on Portola yet?"

"The one that's in the old Firestone tire store? The food must taste like rubber."

"No, no, no. The food is really good. They've got a great bar, too, even a mixologist. People are lining up to get in."

"Mixologist?"

"An expert at mixing drinks."

"You mean a bartender?"

"No, no, this one *creates* drinks. Made me what he calls a Latin Quarter Walkabout."

"I'll take your word for it."

"Sybil, listen." He leans forward, his blue eyes probing hers, a sheen of sweat on his forehead. "You should think about selling this place. I'm serious. With all the redevelopment going on around here, I can find you a buyer in no time and put you in a nice condo downtown, one of those penthouse lofts with stainless steel appliances where you wouldn't have to do anything."

"I need stainless steel appliances less than I need some trendy bistro." She scowls at his untouched cup of coffee.

"Come on. Wouldn't it be great to live in a place that's brand new? Walking distance to the movies, restaurants, Target. I know you love Target."

"I like living on the edge of town." She started thinking about selling when he first brought it up the day after the windstorm, but it's the tenants she worries about. They'd all have to move. And besides, she's owned the cottages on the Old Road since 1971 when her grandpa passed away and she moved in, letting that grease monkey "what's-his-name" come with her, the one who reminded her of Dale.

Memories should be enough to keep her here, the lovers who paraded in and out of her little house over the years, the tenants who brought her turkeys for Christmas, champagne at New Years, treated her to lunch on her birthday, but it's Jamie, she admits now, packing up her kids and taking off without so much as a good-bye, that gives her pause. She misses smart little Lily. The boyness of Collin. She misses Jamie too, her striving to be a good wife, a good mother, someone with a future. And if Sybil sells the place, she won't be here when they come back.

Two days after the storm, the girl's husband, Joel, knocked on Sybil's door. He didn't seem surprised to hear they were gone. Just nodded his head, thinking it over, then said, "Good. Glad they're safe," and asked Sybil if Jamie owed her any money. She told him "no," and was about to ask him where they might've gone, when he turned, and waving his hand over his head, strode through the courtyard to where he'd parked his truck on the Old Road, and took off.

Sybil thought it was strange Joel wasn't more concerned, but since Mars German found a Samsonite suitcase packed with the clothes crushed under the tree, Sybil decided Jamie's exit was planned before the windstorm hit. Maybe she and Joel were meeting up somewhere.

Ian stops yammering. Barks, "Sybil?"

"What?"

"I lost you there for a minute."

"Sorry."

"There's a great place over on Central. Nice view. I could pick up the keys and take you over this morning if you want. Pool, clubhouse, exercise room. Keep that great shape of yours. It would be less lonely. Less work for sure."

She catches him studying her neck where the skin is red and wrinkled. She thinks, he's wondering how long I've got before I keel over. He's hoping I don't have any living relatives.

"You want to get out in front of this, Syb."

*Syb?* Really?

"Once everyone on the Old Road decides to sell, you won't get as good a price. My mother says your neighbors have listed their house."

"Which ones?" It's her turn to stare at him, frowning at the bits of chocolate in the corners of his mouth.

"The Trencher mansion next door."

"Never happen. John Trencher grew up in that place."

"Oh, it's happening. We've got the listing. Just waiting to do some maintenance before putting put up the sign. Look, this is a good thing for everyone. Shops, cafés, that sort of thing. They've got federal funds to revitalize the creek. Make it like the old days."

She yanks the two sides of her robe together at the throat as if clouds blotted out the morning sun. "Sounds like the perfect time to stay put, not sell. Aren't you going to be late for work?"

He shrugs. Stretches his legs, sticking his feet between the vertical bars of the porch railing, his hands behind his head as if he's got nothing better to do than chat up the landlady.

Oh right, she thinks, chatting up the landlady is his work. His mother is behind this. Of course she is.

Sybil stands, begins to gather cups and coffee pot. "Ian, I have work to do."

"Well, think about it. You won't be sorry. I promise I'll take good care of you, Sybil." He pulls himself to his feet and waving good-bye, trots down the porch steps. As he rounds the corner by the carport, he shouts, "Hey, your blue jay ever come back?"

"Not yet, but he will."

"I wouldn't count on it. It's a wild bird. He could be anywhere by now."

Sybil tightens her lips and shivers. The sweet spring breeze is gone.

# Mother and Son

The real estate office, located among trendy shops and restaurants on Central, is cavernous on the inside. Several workstations line one wall, fashionably modern in design, each identical to the other.

On the opposite side, bigger spaces with nicer desks, five in total, sit behind planters with lush foliage. One of these areas belongs to Rita Shane. A sego palm fills the corner window; a Persian carpet covers the floor. Her huge glass desk faces an antique sofa and faux tiger-skin coffee table where a recent copy of *Architectural Digest* has been placed next to her business cards in a gold-leaf tray.

"Ian! There you are." Rita glows at the sight of her son, who presents himself with his usual blend of discomfort and grace. "That suit is amazing. Let me feel the fabric."

He holds out his arm. She slips her slim fingers between his shirt and jacket sleeve. Purrs, "Nice," then gives him what can only be called a "flirtatious" smile.

He pulls away, not quite jerking, says "Mom," and glances around the office to see if anyone is watching. A couple of agents sit at desks, shuffling paperwork, the receptionist chats on the phone, everyone else is out on calls.

"Oh, don't be a goof. I'm just glad I taught you how to dress. You're an asset to my business and I appreciate that. You haven't said anything about my hair."

"Platinum, huh?"

"Almost platinum. Do you like it?"

"Of course I do, Mom. It looks – great."

She kisses the air in his direction and asks, "How'd it go with Sybil this morning."

He throws himself down in the side chair next to her clear glass desk.

"Careful," she says, but smiles big. "You know how much this little treasure cost."

"Then maybe you should've bought mahogany."

She picks up her cell, a shiny new Blackberry, and studies it. "So is Sybil on board?"

"She's not an easy nut to crack."

"But you'll do it, honey. I know that. Just keep at her. Use your charm. I have confidence in you, you know that." She taps something into the phone.

Ian scowls. "I thought I had her this morning, but ..."

"Don't blame yourself. She's a tough old broad. She's lucky to have that man helping with the clean-up. Might be better for us if he wasn't." Her voice slows as she absently swipes the screen. "Who is he anyway, some nephew?"

"No. He's Gus German's son."

Looking up, she beams. "Well, Ian, don't worry about Sybil. Anyone who lives in the same place for a billion years is going to be reluctant, and you are charming, and I'm certain she will eventually give up her shoddy old collection of buildings for something new and shiny and beautiful."

"It's not so bad, you know."

"That's the spirit, sweetie. You'll be out of there soon enough."

"And into that penthouse you promised." He leans forward, rubs his hands, turns to grin at her.

"You'll have your penthouse, darling, just not that one."

He snaps, "What?"

"The offer was just too good to refuse."

"No, no. Don't tell me that."

"Beautiful condos open up all the time. You know that. Have I ever, ever let you down?" She leans across her glass desk, opens her hand, beckons his. He hesitates, then puts his larger one in hers. She squeezes, rubs it with her thumb. Again he casts a look around as a female agent hurries in from outside and drops her Louis Vuitton on her desk across the room.

Rita whispers, all concern, "What's the matter, sweetheart? Are you feeling okay? Does your head hurt? Your tummy?"

"You shouldn't have sold the penthouse without talking to me. You promised, you know."

"I did it for us, Ian, our future." She steps over to him, and leaning down, wraps her arms around his neck. "I'll make sure you get what you want. I always do."

He sits there, staring into the suddenly bustling office as more agents arrive with coffees and clatter, waiting for her arms to let go.

# Father and Son

As sunset streaks his window, Gus German watches the last few minutes of the TV news. Gracie, corgi-husky mix, sits alert at his feet, sweeping her tail along the shag carpet. He ignores the dog because he's learned that making any movement or comment at this time of day will send the animal into paroxysms of impatience. When the old man finally shuts down the TV, he grins at his mutt. "You ready for your walk?"

The path down to the creek is steep, so Gus and the dog take their time, Gracie burying her muzzle in every clump of weeds, every pile of dirt. Boy Scouts have spent hours of community service cleaning up the mess from the January windstorm, all except for the huge eucalyptus that fell over Gus' favorite route. Each afternoon he hopes the tree has been removed and they can go into the clearing where the city recedes behind rustling shrubs, where chittering squirrels and afternoon parrots provide the only other sounds. Gus longs for his Iowa roots, the serenity that comes from acres of endless corn around a stand of cedars, the burble of a stream.

He stops at the fallen eucalyptus, his closed mouth moving in silent frustration. What did he expect? Mounds of debris still wait for city pick-up at curbs along the Old Road.

Gus tugs on Gracie's leash and ambles toward the track edging the flood channel. Riolito Creek used to be a special place to visit, people coming from the mid-west to enjoy the area's warm dry summers. That is, until the Army Corp of Engineers built a dam in Homestead Canyon and lined the streambed with cement and enclosed it with chain-link fencing, changing the natural swell and ebb of the water.

He wished they'd let it be. Sybil claims she played in the creek when she was a girl. Remembers catching trout. Trout! How wonderful, he thinks, if there were trout.

"Dad?" Mars tramps down the trail after Gus, grinning.

The old man mutters to himself, "And now, my day is ruined," as he continues to plod along the wire fence as if he hadn't heard.

"I knew I'd find you here. Hey Gracie, you dog."

"What'd you want, Mars?"

The son's smile disappears. "Thought we'd go out to dinner, you know, since it's your birthday."

"I don't like missing *Wheel of Fortune*." Gus halts. "Besides, why do I wanna go out and eat somebody else's food?"

"For the fun of it?"

"Fun is sitting in my own living room, yelling, 'Time waits for no man' before some doofus shouts it out on TV. Oh, never mind. I got a couple of boxes of Mac-and-Cheese. If you wanna eat, let's eat." He yanks at the leash, and Gracie trips on her short feet as they turn back, heading home.

He feels Mars' eyes boring into his back. In the old days Mars was the one who stomped off, and the old man wouldn't see him for days. And for a second, Gus imagines his boy at fourteen, kicked out of school, and packing a grocery bag with jeans and t-shirts. Gus had let him go then because his second wife didn't like the kid. Didn't want to be responsible for him. And he would be relieved to let him go now, but when he reaches the street, there's Mars trudging up the path after him.

Inside the cottage, Gus fills a saucepan with water and puts it on the stove to boil. Mars opens the fridge and brings out a bottle of wine. He grabs two wine glasses from the cupboard, pours the Sauvignon Blanc, and hands one to Gus who feels the familiar irritation he always feels when his son is around for more than ten minutes.

"I got a job," says Mars.

"What kind of job?" Good, thinks Gus. Don't want you moving in here.

"You know Ian, that guy next door?"

"The shiny penny? You're gonna work for him?"

"His mother. She has people working for her, you know, cleaning up yards, painting, moving furniture. Houses don't sell 'as-is' anymore. The better they look, the more money she makes."

"Well, don't go walking off with anything. One stint in jail is enough. Thank heaven your mother never lived to see that."

Mars stares at him, fists curling, his body stiff and throbbing, just like when he was a boy. "She lived long enough to see you abandon us."

Gus pushes around his son to the pantry. Takes out two blue boxes and sets them on the counter.

Still rigid, Mars asks, "Why do you think I'll never change?"

People don't change, thinks Gus. Whatever his own faults were when he was young, they've magnified with age – impatience, severity, intolerance – and he's too old and too tired to change now. His son won't be any different.

Mars raises his voice. "You want me to go? I'll go."

"No, I don't want you to go." Gus' arm comes up fast to wave off the idea, and Mars flinches. That flinch. The surge of annoyance shooting through Gus requires all his willpower not to turn wave into blow.

The old man shakes himself, pivots quickly to the pan on the stove, lifts the lid and breathes in steam. It takes him a couple moments, frowning at the tiny bubbles forming around the sides, to regain control. If he'd only said "yes" to Mars's dinner invitation to go out, they'd already be seated at some Mexican restaurant, the waitress scribbling down their order. The food would come out pronto and they'd eat, both of them keeping their mouths full, and they'd be paying the bill in a half hour or so. Mars would drop him back home, and Gus would tell him "don't bother coming in," and off the kid would go. But none of this is possible now. He should've known.

Mars straightens his shoulders, takes a gulp of wine, and settles against the counter. After a moment, he says, "Did Sybil ever hear from that woman with the two kids?"

"Not that she's ever said." He nudges Mars aside to get at the boxes of Mac-and-Cheese. Rips off their cardboard tops.

"Where'd she take off to?" Mars swallows more wine.

"I don't know. Back to her mother, I guess."

"Sybil said she doesn't have a mother."

"Then why're you asking me?"

"I'm just making conversation."

Gus glances at the clock over the stove. Too early for *Wheel*, thinks happy damn birthday to me, then checks the water. Almost there. Good enough. He dumps in both packs of macaroni and stirs it.

"So Dad," says Mars. "What'll you do when Sybil sells the cottages?"

Gus pales. "Sell? I don't wanna move."

"You won't have a choice. Everything on this block is going to be sold, but Mrs. Shane doesn't want anyone to feel put out."

"Put out?"

"That's what she said. She wants to be fair. Which is why I'm giving you a heads up. Since she's my boss now, you have an in: me. My birthday present to you."

"You're my 'in'? For what?"

"Whatever you want. A new place, a better place."

"What about the other tenants?"

"She's happy to help them too. She wants everything to go smooth as silk."

Gus gives his son a hard look, turns away, back to the water and the pasta boiling over and hissing on the stove. "I bet she does."

# The Diner

Charmaine Martin can't stand the chaos of remodelling another minute, and flees to the old-fashioned diner up on Portola. Not her usual kind of place, four or five tables and a long counter, all warm wood with a shake roof hanging over the griddle where a chubby, yellow-haired cook grills burgers, cheese sandwiches, and tuna melts, but the distance is doable and she hopes a thick icy malt will settle her stomach and the walk will loosen her back.

She didn't expect to feel pain so early in her pregnancy, but hunching over her computer for hours always puts a strain on her back. Besides, Sam's working late, over-scheduling his days, taking on new patients, covering for the other podiatrist's vacation, because house paint, new toilets, and a baby on the way have emptied their savings. She doesn't mind him gone so much, not really. All his hammering and sawing makes it hard for her to work. She has her own job designing webpages to focus on.

She turns up Portola Street from the Old Road and notices the stop sign at the corner hasn't yet been replaced. Makes her think of the stick characters she draws. Funny stick characters. She'd use brick red (#CB4154) for the head and silver (#CDC5C2) for skinny body bent at the waist, doing what, barfing? Medium green (#8A9A5B). She smiles for the first time in hours.

The website she's working on now is for the new baby store across the street from the diner. Maybe she'll stop there first and talk to the owner about the logo – Charmaine wants to tweak it a bit – but what she really wants is that strawberry malt.

It feels good to be out in the air, the days finally growing longer. The spare bedroom is jammed with unpacked boxes, her computer on a card table stuck in a windowless corner, and she's worried about how she'll manage when the baby comes. Sam says she can get things done while the baby sleeps, but what if the baby doesn't sleep?

She glances in the window of the store, noticing the delicately knit caps for newborns, the onesies, the sleep sacques, and blankets on display, in soft green, pale aqua, daffodil yellow. She steps close to better see a tiny pink polka dot dress trimmed in lace. She touches the glass with her fingertips. The owner looks up and waves. Charmaine waves back and walks on. Maybe she isn't in the mood to talk.

There's an auto body shop across the street next to the diner and on the other side is a sleek new café and bar, like something you might see downtown, not in this neighborhood. She and Sam should eat there some night. The gentrification of Portola was one of the reasons they bought the bungalow. It would be a good investment. She'd talked Sam into it, her spirits lifting.

The only customer in the diner is a man sitting at one of the tables, his back to the door. The cook puts a bowl of soup in front of him.

Charmaine slides in at the counter.

"Chocolate or strawberry?" Smiling, the cook wipes his hands on a towel tucked at his waist.

"Strawberry with lots of whipped cream."

"You're not afraid of losing your figure, are you?"

"Not a bit." She doesn't say anything else. She feels uncomfortable sharing the news that her belly will be expanding rapidly over the next few months, and she doesn't show much yet, though today she feels bloated. Maybe she shouldn't have a malt, she thinks, but the cook is already scooping in the frozen strawberries.

She waits for the blender to stop whirring, her back twinging with pain. It's only tension, but she wishes now she'd crawled into bed.

It's quiet in the diner, still early for the after-work crowd, and the man at the table is looking over his shoulder at her. She senses his stare and glances around, noticing his nylon running pants, the kind with the stripe down the leg, black on blue. He's clean shaven, cropped hair, kind of handsome, she thinks, yet there's a crystalline hardness to his eyes.

Lowering her head, she focuses on the malt now in front of her. Jabs the straw into the thick liquid, softening it, so she can drink it down quickly, but she's lost her appetite. She digs in her pocket for the twenty-dollar bill she brought with her, tosses it on the counter, slides off the stool, and bolts out the door, her hand back in her pocket, feeling the warm metal of her house key.

# The Man at the Table

He needs the diner empty of customers. The cook doesn't count, but this woman shouldn't be here. She's an unwelcome intrusion, a distraction. He pins his eyes to her back, willing her to sense his presence, understand his need for privacy, and when she turns around, he glares. He can tell she's trying to ignore him, her head bent close to her malt, ramming that straw up and down, but he's unnerved her, and before long, she throws money on the counter, and races out.

Two long months have passed since he jogged along the Old Road back to his car against a hard wind, eyes watering, ears ringing, his unzipped sweatshirt snapping behind him. He'd collapsed into the driver's seat and shoved his hand into his pants while the storm's fury rattled around him.

He remembers vividly the mineral smell, the lit brilliance of agitated air, the burn in his chest when he breathed. And Jamie, her silhouette in the window, dark against amber. A growl escapes his throat.

In the deep hours of each night, with his skinny wife next to him, he conjures Jamie in her little cottage, waiting for him. She aches as he aches, but understands the necessity of delay, of denial, the absolute desideratum of not giving in until the last moment when the sky will finally open and swallow them both.

His fingers twitch. It's almost time. He feels it coming.

But not yet. This is as close as he'll allow himself. It's better this way. It's always better to deny.

He dips the spoon into vegetable soup, brings it to his lips. Cold.

# A Passing

Outside in the brisk March air, warming her hands on her coffee mug, Sybil waits for Mars to show. He's been less reliable these days, ever since he started working for Ian's mother. The tree guys came a week ago, turning the fallen oak into firewood, grinding out the stump. Makes her sad to think nothing is left of that grand old tree but a lumpy hole in the ground, and after Mars hauls away the last traces of Jamie's cottage, smooths out the dirt, and throws some grass seed around, even that will be gone.

A shiny white car pulls to the curb. A large man climbs out and strides toward her. Slipping on her glasses, she recognizes Louisa Renke's son, and from the grim set of his mouth, she knows why he's here.

"Mr. Renke," she says as he approaches. "Not bad news, I hope."

His eyes shift from the debris at the front of the property to his mother's cottage. He swallows, and says, "She passed away yesterday. It was okay. In her sleep. She was ready."

Sybil scurries down her porch steps, puts her hand on his forearm and squeezes. "I'm so, so sorry."

A muffled sob erupts from the big man. Everyone, she thinks, no matter who they are, comes to a moment when something burrows into their gut and wrings out such a sound.

"Can I help with anything?" she asks.

He doesn't answer; she's patient. She doesn't let go of his arm. Then he places his hand on hers, and asks, "Will you help me to find something for her to wear?"

His words summon to mind a casket, rosewood maybe, satin trim – Ray has money – with Louisa's face softened in death, carefully applied make-up mocking her with blush.

"Of course," she says, as they walk arm and arm in silence across to number 3, hesitating for a moment before mounting the stairs.

"I'll keep paying rent until I get all her affairs in order." He slides his key into the lock of his mother's front door. "Through the next couple months at least. Is that enough time for you to find another tenant?"

"That'll work out fine." If the Prentiss family comes back, they'll need a place to stay. She's not so sure about Joel, though. It bothers her how Jamie up and took the kids, not waiting for her husband to come home, not even saying good-bye.

Regardless, she'll keep it empty for a while. And no need to rebuild the front bungalow. Clear the space instead, she thinks. Plant the grass. Build an arbor.

Louisa Renke's house feels forsaken despite the crocheted throw over the arm of the sofa, the stack of crossword puzzles on the coffee table next to the remote. Poor Louisa, swept away to the hospital after her heart attack, deposited into a nursing home, never coming home again, never able to say good-bye to her things.

Sybil follows Ray into the bedroom where a green chenille bedspread takes her back to when she was a girl. She had a similar one in pale pink. She brushes her hand along the nubby fabric, a faint smile flashing on her lips.

From the closet, Ray pulls out a stiff, old-fashioned pantsuit with manly shoulder pads, an outfit Sybil had never seen the old woman wear.

"This is how I remember her," he says. "In this suit, or one like it, kissing me on the forehead as she dashed out the

210

door for work. I remember the back of it better than the front."

"She worked at Bradshaw's Department Store, didn't she?"

"Advertising, downtown headquarters. She rode those copywriters like a trail boss. Whipped 'em hard. That's what she used to say. I guess no one would get that today."

"I get it. I used to watch *Rawhide*," Sybil says.

Ray grins at this. "Me too. Mother was a pistol. Women didn't work a man's job back then, when other women were hanging laundry on clotheslines."

"I hung laundry on clotheslines," says Sybil, and for a moment she remembers herself shaking out damp sheets, pegging them to a rope strung between the back of her house and a lone hackberry tree. "But I wanted to be like your mother."

"I guess she'd choose this suit to be buried in," says Ray.

"Anything in there you'd prefer?"

Ray looks up, as if this thought never occurred to him. He revisits the closet.

A door slams outside and Sybil tiptoes into the living room to peek out the front door. Mars German strolls toward the remains of Jamie's ruined house while $10-an-hour laborers jump off the back of a rusty pick-up truck. Good, she thinks. He knows what to do, and leaving the door ajar to let in fresh air, she returns to the bedroom.

Ray holds up a summer print dress with yellow, red, and aqua bouquets scattered across a white background, scooped neck, cap sleeves, a red belt cinching the waist, and a full pleated skirt. His face is shining.

"Oh!" Sybil gives a little gasp, the dress so unexpectedly pretty.

"I only remember her wearing it once. We spent the day together, shopping at her store, maybe it was my birthday, I think, and then we had lunch in the Tea Room. I'd forgotten that. The store had a Tea Room."

211

"Then this is the dress she should wear," says Sybil. "So you can remember her in this dress, and remember that time. A funeral is for the living, Ray, not the dead."

He ponders this as if he's still a little frightened his mother will disapprove, scrunching his eyebrows. Sybil studies her fingers. It's none of her business. He has to decide this for himself.

"I'm not sure it'll fit her. She's so much smaller now."

"They can take care of that. They do that kind of thing all the time."

He lays the dress carefully on the bed. Spreads out the skirt. "I didn't think she had this dress anymore. You know, my wife, ex-wife, is the one who helped her move in here. I was too busy."

"Your mother must have understood that."

"You're right. She did. If nothing else, she was proud of my success." He straightens up. "She's going to need shoes. The guy at the mortuary said a lot of people forget the shoes."

He rummages through the closet, comes up holding a pair of black orthopaedic sandals.

"No." Sybil shakes her head. "Never."

"That's all she's got."

Sybil stares down at her own feathery satin slippers. Too floozy. The rest of her shoes are like Louisa's, designed for comfort, not beauty. Then she remembers. "Hold on. I'll be right back." She hurries outside. Feeling a little foolish and way too old to be streaking across the yard, she waves at Mars. He hollers "Hello" as she heads into her garage at the back of the property.

It's dark inside and cool. Sybil flips on a light and starts shifting boxes, searching for the few labelled "Prentiss." Amazing to her how few belongings Jamie and her little family had. Toys, of course, a TV and VCR, and clothing. The furniture and most of the kitchen goods had been rented from Sybil, but she'd packed up what was theirs, just in case.

Would Jamie mind this gesture of Sybil's, this raiding of her shoes? Sybil doesn't think so. She opens another box and at its bottom, finds what she's looking for, a pair of white high heels with red leather detailing on the back.

Pulling herself to her feet, Sybil smiles. She wants to see that look on Ray Renke's face again, the almost childlike remembrance in his eyes of a day well spent with his mother. She knows that Louisa would be pleased, even though the old woman would always wave away any discussion of her son with the simple comment, "That boy. He deserves a better mother than me."

# Detectives

The female cop wears black: slacks, tank top, a chunky necklace and silver belt. She isn't heavy exactly, but she isn't slim. Short, fair skin, freckles, Detective Ross is a ginger.

Sybil, sitting down on the sofa, clasps her hands together in her lap. "You said Joel reported them missing?"

"I did," says Detective Hierra, khakis, white shirt, and a brown sport coat, no tie. "So Mrs. Prentiss took her two children and disappeared during the night, is that right?"

"Not during the night. They stayed here with me after the tree fell, and they didn't leave until late morning."

"What did she say when she left?" Ross asks. "What did she take with her?"

"She didn't say anything. I was out front on the sidewalk talking to one of my tenants, Ian Shane, and his mother. Jamie and the kids must've gone out the back door to the carport and left. She didn't take much with her if anything. I have what we salvaged packed up in the garage."

Hierra says, "We'd like to take a look once we're done here."

"Of course."

"Weren't you worried when she went off like that? Did you report it to the police?" Ross again.

"I called them that night, around nine when it seemed like they weren't coming back, but whoever I talked to at the police station said it was too soon for them to get involved,

214

then Joel, her husband, came around the next day, and he assured me everything was fine. She'd probably gone to her aunt's. He gave me the impression he was headed up there and wasn't worried. I – I ..."

"What, Mrs. Howard? Had Jamie Prentiss confided in you?" asks Ross.

"Not really. It's just ..." Sybil searches for the right words. "I had a sense that – and she never said a word to me – but one of the reasons I was still – *am* still – worried is that I felt she didn't exactly leave. She fled."

"What made you think that? Wasn't she happy in her marriage, did she ever say she was abused?"

Sybil dips her head, a sudden rush of doubt coming over her. "I watched the kids when she went to class, and we talked some, but she never opened up and I never saw any signs of physical abuse, but that doesn't mean anything. I don't think she was happy. He was never around, she was always short of money, they argued a lot. He always tried to come off as so successful, but there was nothing to show that was true."

The detectives shoot glances at each other.

Hierra says, "He says he's spent the last couple months trying to track them. He went everywhere he thought they might go, up to Oregon where her aunt lives and back to New Hampshire where she came from. Couldn't find any trace of her, so he decided he should come to us."

"We hoped that perhaps she'd talked to you," Ross says, "or that you might know of some friends he doesn't know about."

"She was going to school, taking classes at the community college, but I don't think she ever mentioned anyone, except her instructor."

"Do you know his name?"

"I don't."

"We can find out. We'll see if she has a friend in class. Is there anything else you can tell us that might help us to find her?"

"She was a quiet person, kept to herself, but she had good intentions. She had what we used to call spunk."

# Chez Shane

Rita Shane lives where the rich live, on wide avenues marching up into the hills or martialled along the flats, "Chez Shane" balancing on a ridge above downtown, facing west with a killer view. Tall buildings in the next town, eight miles away, press against the setting sun, a lit swimming pool sparkles blue-green fifteen feet beyond plate glass, and in between, the hills are empty darkness. Mars stands in his boxer shorts, a glass of wine in his hand.

"You can stay." Rita behind him. "No reason to go back to that ratty motel of yours."

"You seemed to like it the first couple times." He doesn't turn around as she presses against him, her naked breast hot against his back.

"That was fun." She mouths the words on his skin, then nips with her teeth, not hard, but hard enough. Breath escapes from his throat.

He says, "You liked the bar too."

"I did."

"And your bed."

"Yes." Her fingers slip inside his boxers, and he turns, his hand firm on the small of her back pulling her against his stiffness, pressing down until her legs give, and he lowers her and enters her, as they collapse onto cold marble tiles.

She'd flirted with him and he'd flirted back, and then she'd sucked the dirt from under his fingernails and he'd pushed her against the urinal at the dive bar down on the wrong end of Central.

"When you say stay, do you mean *stay?*" he asks when they are splayed side by side on Rita Shane's marble.

"Why not?"

Outside the wall of glass, wavelets skitter across the swimming pool, distant lights prick the black, and inside, the stone is cold, unyielding.

# Flipping Out

Charmaine Martin snorts at the mushroom smell of wet grout and curses her husband. White tile! Not even subway! Didn't she force him to watch hours of pre-recorded HGTV just to avoid this kind of mistake? Marble equals updated. Tile, not so much. And still, he has the guy install it behind her back, while she's at his sister's shitty baby shower!

She pivots away, can't stand the sight of it, and bangs her toe. A tool, of course, one of Sam's. Left on the floor, not put away. She stoops and snatches the hammer, its wood handle smooth with age. Rust speckles the worn head, the curved claw. She tosses it hard onto the counter and it lands with a crack. She looks. Grins. A broken square of tile. Good. Serves him right.

But more than this is broken. Everything's broken. How she'd loved this house when they were scraping together the down payment, when all she saw was potential. Now she's overwhelmed with mold snaking through the basement, termites camped in the attic, the plumber who fell through the dining room ceiling, the gush of water that followed him down. Funny at the time, but the aftermath, the damage, the money, the delay.

She stalks into the bedroom where an air mattress fills one corner and throws herself onto the puddle of sheets. She wishes it wasn't Saturday, wishes Sam wasn't outside chopping up what's left of the sycamore that fell last

January. She wants to wallow and he hates to see her wallow. But wouldn't that punish him for his thoughtlessness? How he tricked her while she was off witnessing his sister's glowing happiness? Is wallowing enough?

A thought makes her shiver. She knows she can't resist this urge. Doesn't want to.

In the bathroom, she lifts the hammer above her shoulder, catches sight of her face in the mirror. Her cheeks are flushed, her eyes glassy, a thick strand of brown hair bisects her face. She bends down, runs a hand roughly from the back of her scalp to the top, then tosses her head. Yes. This is who she is now, the powerful, childless woman in the glass, wielding her weapon, and smirking, she smacks the hammer down, shatters each shiny new tile one by one. Chips of ceramic fly, skidding across the counter onto the floor as she moves faster and faster.

"Charmaine!"

She spins around and there's Sam, blocking the doorway, face spotted with dirt, hair sweat-damp, body odor rolling off him. She has a right to show anger. A right to put him in his place. She says, "See what happens when you don't listen to me? When I say marble, I mean *marble*." She holds up the hammer and moving toward him, everything a blur until she's close enough to feel his heat, close enough to experience a tremor of fear – has she gone too far this time? But he steps out of her way, back into the bedroom. Her heart pounds and her foot falters, but she keeps walking.

Out the front door she runs, exhilarated with triumph, the sun vying with rain, the devil beating his wife, as her mother used to say. Trembling, she pitches the hammer onto the lawn, watches it thud, then strides past Sam's tidy stack of cut wood and onto the sidewalk.

She doesn't know where she's going, but she can't go back inside. Not yet. She looks up and down the Old Road and spies a neighbor, that old man who's always walking his dog, coming up from the creek. She glances around, and hurries toward the only place out of the open, through the peeling blue gate and up the long walkway to the Trencher mansion next door.

Although most yards along the Old Road tend to be scruffy, this one, is filled with knee-high weeds and no attempt has been made to clean the mess left by the storm. The owners have gone overseas, England, she thinks, or Wales, and won't be back, according to Sam who, unlike her, enjoys the occasional chat with neighbors. The house is appealing in spite of dead bushes, crumbling paint, and the broken window on the second floor. She loves the sprawl of it and the arched entryway built like the entrance into a Moorish fort. This is a place just waiting to be flipped, much more potential than her own little bungalow with its tacky kitchen and wormy wood.

Sam. Is he following her? She can't tell and she's afraid to look. She will explode if she has to endure, even for a second, the sympathy in his eyes. She wishes he'd just grab her and shake her, throw her on the floor, kick her in the belly, and leave. Damn him. Damn him.

The front door has one of those key boxes on it. She steals up the walkway, and with a glance at the empty street, she checks the box. The contraption is shut and locked, doesn't yield to her tug. She fingers each dial as if she's cracking a safe but to no avail. She stamps her foot, tastes blood in her mouth.

She cuts over to the driveway and into the unkempt back yard, surveying the lower windows, grinning when she sees French doors leading from a cracked cement patio into the house. A glance yields an assortment of fallen branches the right size for her use. In this moment, she considers the January windstorm a blessing, sent to her by a forgiving god who loves her and only her. Making up perhaps for what he's taken away. She hefts one limb and then another and selects the one that most resembles a baseball bat.

Reflected in the double doors her image is divided into twelve square panes, and like in the bathroom mirror, she rejoices in the powerful figure she sees. "Towanda on a rampage" passes through her head from some forgotten movie, and with the end of the branch she breaks the glass, one pane splintering at a time. She reaches in and tries the door, but it's bolted. The branch now a battering ram, she smashes out each slat of wood – bam – bam – bam! – until the hole is large enough for her to stoop inside.

In the late afternoon light, she can barely make out the table and chairs in the center of the room. She searches for a light switch, finds one, flicks it back and forth. No lights come on, but down the hall, rosy sunlight draws her into the huge living room. Hardwood floors, a fireplace at the far end, its gorgeous tile smudging her fingertips with soot. She sees herself emptying the house of its hideous furniture, pulling down the heavy velvet curtains, restoring the vaulted ceiling, filling the rooms with antiques.

Her hand runs over worn mahogany as she climbs the winding staircase, reminding her of the hammer handle, polished by years of contact with skin. If they owned this house, she'd take up the threadbare carpeting, put down a Persian runner, add those brass bars that fit neatly at the back of each step. She could work wonders here.

At the top, on the large landing, the setting sun stains the stucco walls red, and Charmaine hesitates, as if restrained by a ghostly hand. In the distance, Sam calls her name, and grimacing, she steps into the nearest bedroom.

She knows what kind of room this is, a mobile motionless in the darkening afternoon, a zoo of stuffed animals lining a window seat, and the crib that she could touch if she only would. She can't move except for breath, her heart shattering like white ceramic tile and twelve square panes of glass.

# Hydrangeas

The broken tiles in the bungalow's bathroom have been removed but not replaced. Neither Sam nor Charmaine suggests repairing the damage. Every morning before work, he brushes his teeth, washes his face, shaves, leaving water spots and stubble scattered across the bare mortar. Charmaine remains in the waterbed, legs pulled to her chest, facing the wall.

This morning Sam's in a hurry and knocks over a bottle of men's cologne. He scrapes away the glass, and lets out a yowl. Blood bubbles up, and he shoves his cut hand under the faucet and cranks up the water. "Damn it!"

He glances over his shoulder, thinking Charmaine will be there, asking him what's wrong, offering to help, but the doorway remains empty.

"God *damn* it." Bloody dots and commas land on the counter and in the sink. He studies the slash. Red beads pop up and flow. He sticks it under the water again, calls out, "Charmaine?"

When he checks again, the bleeding has slowed. He wraps his hand in a hand towel, holds it tight with the other, and walks into the murky bedroom. From the slits of light in the blinds, he can make out her form on the bed, the back of her head, the slight movement of her legs.

Impatience tightens his chest, throbs at his temples, forcing him to bite down hard on the inside of his lip to stay in control. This has got to stop, he thinks. She doesn't move.

Sighing, he returns to the bathroom for antiseptic and bandage.

Slams the front door when he leaves.



He comes home late with huge blue hydrangeas and a rotisserie chicken from the grocery store and finds Charmaine at her computer in the spare room. She's playing a game and doesn't hear him. He watches her as she listlessly rearranges brightly-colored candies on the screen.

He says softly, "Charmaine."

She whips around, startled. "Oh."

He hands the flowers to her, leans down, and kisses her forehead. She stares at the bouquet. He puts the chicken behind the computer and sits on a packing box close to her. Touches her hand. When she looks up, her eyes are wet, and he moves toward her and pulls her to him, the flowers crushed between them.

He whispers, "I'm sorry. So so so sorry."

She breaks away first, a weak smile on her lips. "Let me get up."

He moves his legs and she walks past him, out of the spare room and into the kitchen. He follows, bringing the chicken. Her back is to him, the flowers on the counter, water running.

He says, "I can make a salad and then we can talk?"

She rips the plastic from the flowers. "Talk?"

"I was thinking we should consider selling the house." Opening the refrigerator, he removes a head of rusty lettuce.

"Why?" Her tone is flat, and her hands still.

"It's a money pit."

"A money pit?"

He puts the lettuce on the counter, inclines his head so he can at least see her profile. "Don't you think we should do that, considering?"

"Considering what?" she snaps.

"This damn house is much more than we bargained for, the repairs are through the roof, and the stress. I feel it and I know you feel it."

"I'm fine." Back to the hydrangeas, she separates them and lines them up on their sides on the bottom of the sink.

"Charmaine."

He grabs her arm, but she yanks it away, growls, "I don't want to sell this house."

"But —"

"I don't want to do it."

"Okay. I thought you'd be relieved." He backs away and begins peeling the sticker off the chicken container, glances up at the sound of a motor. The faucet is on full blast, and the flowers, stuffed into the garbage disposal, are spinning wildly.

"What are you doing?" he screams, though he knows he shouldn't.

Shock pales her face and she quickly flicks off the disposal. Sam pulls her close, almost lifting her off the floor, his mantra, "So sorry. So sorry. So sorry."

# The Return

He often eats at the diner on Portola in the afternoon, sits at the same table, orders vegetable soup. He sips it slowly, rolling the bits of potato and carrot, the slivers of beef on his tongue, savoring each texture, each flavor. He hasn't ventured any closer to the Old Road than this, but today, he won't go to the diner.

He wakes up late, Jamie's face coming to him, clear and sharp, her tongue pressed against her front teeth, hazel eyes wary, standing in his classroom, handing in her late assignment, her voice low and throaty, making her excuses. She isn't beautiful, merely pretty – and sad. He lusts for sad. And she isn't coy, never flirting, but he knows she's holding back, as disciplined as he, kindred spirits. He imagines his finger tracing a line from her mouth, down along her nipples, first one, then the other, slowly to her cunt. Alone in his bed for once, his body responds, the mind a remarkable instrument of persuasive creation.

Later he stands naked in front of the mirror inspecting his sandy hair, coarse and gray above his ears, the deep crease around each side of his mouth, his neck mottled pink, but not bad. He's lean, wiry, his daily five-mile runs assuring no fat.

In the shower, he soaps each crevice of his body, rinsing in water so hot he grits his teeth to stay beneath the spray. He dresses with care, a thin white t-shirt, running shorts, his lime green Saucony's. Again he stares in the mirror, this time his cheeks a healthy rose, eyes sharp and gleaming.

He luxuriates in the silence of his house, walking from empty room to empty room, straightening a stack of books, wiping a smudge off the dining room door, polishing the faucet, wife and daughter halfway across the continent visiting his in-laws. So today it can begin. He'll stop by. Tell Jamie he's been worried. Could he take her out for coffee or dinner? Perhaps to the new upscale restaurant near the diner? Not to pester her about dropping out, but rather to assure her she can count on him in any way she needs, reinstatement at the community college, mentoring, money. He sees her potential.

It took everything he had when it appeared she wasn't coming back in January not to head to the Old Road, break down her door, and demand to know what she was up to. That was one thought, the easy thought, and it made him calm, but the other thought, that she was gone, that he should make certain she was still there, titillated. She was married with two kids: what if her husband changed jobs, what if they'd moved out of the county? He had these thoughts before and has them now, but that's the point, isn't it? To stay away, leave it up to fate, live with the denial, and perhaps in the end, thwart his darkest desires? The withholding, the privation of possibility is exactly the point.

He yearns for Jamie more than anyone before, delaying the endgame longer, embracing the task of waiting. He's kept her on the edge of his mind, his pleasure in the denial of his urges, a tension created by his unfulfilled physical need. He's survived on his mental projection of possibilities, refusing to give in. It's this discipline that has been his most exquisite torture.

*

He parks exactly where he parked in January, on Portola, east of the Tudor on the corner of the Old Road. This time, however, instead of jogging along the sidewalk, he indulges in one more excruciating delay before yielding to his bliss. He's never gone this long before without giving up, giving in, ruining something that could have been perfect.

He crosses to the creek side and scrambles into the arroyo where the afternoon sun sharpens the leaves of trees and glints off the thread of water at the bottom of the concrete channel. His heart bangs against his ribs, his body buzzes as he struts along the chain-link. In this wildish place on the edge of town, smelling of grass and dirt, he prepares himself for his final move.

A twist to his ankle shakes him out of his trance and tumbles him against something rough and hard, scraping his hand as he tries to catch his fall. He looks up and gapes because his brain can't compute what he sees: a knot of snakes bristling from a giant head in the weeds along the path, its Medusa shadow stretching behind, his own shadow leaping away. It takes him a moment to recognize the stump of a eucalyptus, torn from the ground and abandoned on its side, its snakes nothing but curling roots.

He tries to laugh at himself, but the sound is forced, bitter. He spits out "Fool. Idiot. Jerk-off!" and kicks at the stump, misses. Wheeling around, he stomps away, up the path to the Old Road.

All these months, he's taken pleasure in denying himself, thinking of her as he watched his female students waiting in the hall before class, brushing past them without quite touching, venturing down the rows of desks while he lectured, standing close enough to feel their heat, but never more than that.

The sun begins its slant behind him, sweat beads his forehead. At the top, on the verge along the Old Road, he forces himself to lean over, catch his breath, and prolongs his moment of perfect anticipation until a shudder of need forces him to look up.

"No." He closes his eyes.

Opens them. "No."

On the night of the windstorm, Jamie stood in the window of a cottage across the Old Road, but now, there's no woman in the window. There's no window, no cottage. Only a lumpy mound of grass remains.

How did this happen? He crosses the road and studies the yard. Then he knows, the windstorm that uprooted oaks, pines, camphors. He sways a little remembering that gale, what it had given him, the storm, the woman, the discipline. And then took away. He'd denied himself because of the rules, his rules. And he'd lasted five months because then, everything would be in place. His family gone. She would be ready. He would be ready. And the endgame was always worth it.

All those months of deprivation just to gape at a hole in the ground? He moves a hand to his crotch, fingers himself through the cloth of his shorts, then stops. This *isn't* how the game is played.

His growing anger pushes him to cross the road, a horn blasts, and he jumps back as a Mini Cooper swerves to miss him. He chases after the car, shaking his fist, his blood rising as if ready to burst through his scalp. Then he stops, twists toward the creek, throws himself down the path, feet kicking up dust, eyes blind, gaining momentum until he runs headlong into the chain-link fence at the bottom.

A howl escapes from his chest and he hangs onto the links as his body sags. He stays, convulsed with tears, until the sound of distant laughter rouses him. He pulls himself up and stumbles along the trail, limping at first, unstable and unable to control the side-to-side lolling of his head in despair.

Adrenaline propels him home, desperate for the safety of his empty house where he can deal with the devastating loss of Jamie.

# Visitor

She hears the creak on the front porch before the knock, so she puts the string of beads she's working back onto the tray and removes the magnifying glasses strapped around her head. When the knock sounds a second time, harder, Sybil pushes her chair away from the dining room table, fluffs her salt and pepper hair, and opens the door.

The man standing on her welcome mat is smiling at her, eyes bright, head arched back, his hand jingling keys in the pocket of his slacks. He says, "I was wondering what happened to the woman who lives in the front cottage? The one that doesn't seem to be there anymore?"

"And who are you?"

He says, "I teach psychology at the community college. Jamie Prentiss was a student of mine."

"Oh, yes. She mentioned you. She said you were one of the better adjunct instructors there."

"She did? That was sweet of her. They call us 'freeway fliers' because we teach classes at two or three schools. Makes it harder to connect, but Jamie and I, we had a rapport. Please, I'm concerned. What happened?"

Sybil waves toward the rattan chairs on the porch, says, "Sit, please. Let's talk."

He gestures for her to sit first, which she does. He scans the courtyard, the empty grass where Jamie's cottage used to stand, a sycamore across the Old Road. The keys in his pocket clink. Then he nods, and joins her at the little table.

The sun in its western arc disappears behind a cloud, the light fading as if on a dimmer switch.

"I happened to come by this way yesterday and saw Jamie's house was gone. I was shocked. She's not taking my class this semester so I had no idea."

"You visited her before?"

"No. She'd told me where she lived and, I don't know, I guess I just remembered, and then was shocked to see nothing there. What happened?"

"An oak tree crashed onto her house during the windstorm back in January."

"She wasn't in it, was she? She wasn't —"

"They were in there, they were rattled — we all were — but they weren't hurt."

"Where did she — they go?"

"Didn't the police talk to you about this?"

The keys jingle. "The police? Why?"

"I'm afraid I sent them your way. They came to find out what I knew about Jamie, if she had any friends. I mentioned you because, well, frankly, she doesn't have any friends that I know of."

"So what are you saying?"

"They went missing the next day, she and the kids."

"Went missing? How? Why?"

"I don't know. Her husband tried to find her, then reported her disappearance."

"I never saw the cops. Not that I could have told them anything. The only conversations I had with her were brief, right after class." He stands up, grimaces. "I almost wish the cops *had* talked to me. It would have saved me the shock. She was a good student. An earnest student. Well, I'm sure she's fine, she and her family."

"But how did you know which cottage was hers? I mean, I understand she said she lived in the cottages, but —"

He pivots away, trots down the porch steps. At the bottom, he peers up at Sybil, his eyes marble-like, a bleak

232

cobalt. He says, "I think I mentioned in class I jogged along the creek and she said she lived on the Old Road, and someone else asked if it was by that big old Spanish house, and she said next door, the cottage in front. So anyway, thanks for the info. Glad she wasn't hurt."

Sybil watches him stride to the sidewalk, turn left, and disappear behind the eugenias.

# By Chance

Charmaine tells herself she's going up to the baby store to talk to the owner about the website. She's trying to put herself – her mind at least – back to where it was before she was pregnant, before the debate between she and Sam raged: she argued "yes" she was ready for a baby. He argued too much was going on. They're young. Thirty-two is young. And she sees now that he was right. The fact she lost the baby is proof, isn't it?

Now Sam wants to try again. Make another baby. Lots of women lose their first, he says. But she doesn't want him near her, his hands on her hands, let alone all over her in bed. Not yet. She tells him she needs to heal, the scraping irritated her uterus, not to mention what it did to her heart.

After Sam heads off to the office this morning, she remains cocooned in the sheets until 10, drifting in and out of sleep, sometimes thinking about her client at the baby store who's been patient about her logo and website, but will probably fire her soon if she doesn't pull the project together. Then she rolls over, thinking she really doesn't give a shit. She's content in this tiny bedroom, on its uncomfortable air mattress, with the sound of termites chewing away in the attic.

She dozes off and dreams of stick figure babies in cartoon versions of baby boy shorts, sailor shirts, blue caps, baby girls in cotton print dresses, ruffled and smocked, with matching diaper covers. A whole row of tottering babies, pinning up the letters of the store's name on a clothesline, wild flowers sprouting out of the poles on either side. She could redraw the actual clothes each new season. Then she realizes she's awake, and planning what she will do, not dreaming any more. She tosses away the covers, showers for the first time in days.

Walking up Portola, she notices how bright the early afternoon light is, how the breeze against her face brings with it the smells of summer grass and the waxy white blooms of the pittosporum trees overhead.

She peeks inside the baby shop, where the owner is unpacking a carton at the counter, plastic wrap on the floor at her feet, a soft pastel quilt unfolded on a nearby display table, lambs and wolf cubs tumbling together.

Charmaine smiles, and then loses the smile.

A reflection in the glass shows the outline of a person. Hesitantly, she turns and recognizes the man who had stared at her the last time she'd gone into the diner, the one with the crystalline eyes.

# The Trencher Mansion

Before crossing the Old Road to the creek side, Gus waits for a couple cars to rumble by. Gracie, meantime, meanders into the newly planted star jasmine beneath the Shane Realty "For Sale" sign, the grand old house finally on the market.

"Come on, girl." He tugs her leash, and notices the property's low blue gate, usually latched, gapes open. In the dim evening light, he squints at the front door, but it's closed, a realtor's lockbox visible in the light from a lantern next to the driveway. All the windows are dark. Kids, of course. Nothing more appealing than an abandoned house.

Gus pulls the gate shut, noticing, even in the growing darkness, the still weedy yard, the scattered debris from January's storm. Maelstroms last winter, polar vortexes back east, now severe drought in the west? "The gods," mutters Gus, "are angry."

A man in a white jacket strides down the sidewalk, aiming for Gus, setting off Gracie, who yelps and strains at her leash. The old man pulls her in and steps out of the way, but the man — the podiatrist or chiropractor, Gus can't remember which kind of fake doctor he is, stops and begs, "Have you seen my wife, maybe on your walk?"

"No, haven't seen anyone. Anything wrong?" The dog barks again and hides behind Gus' legs.

"My front door's open, her purse is on the kitchen table, but I can't find her," the man says. "We're supposed to see my family tonight."

"You sure she's not taking a nap. Gracie, heel. You're a doctor, right? From the bungalow?"

"Podiatrist. Sam Martin. Thanks." The man pivots away, yanks open the gate, speeds up the walkway of the Trencher house.

"Hey!" Gus hollers. "You can't go in there. Nobody's home." The old man shambles after him, Gracie trotting ahead, Gus' heart pulling on his chest, his mind jumbled with images of the wife dead inside, the man breaking a window, the mansion going up in flames.

"This is private property." Gus puffs toward the backyard. He hears the younger man calling, "Charmaine!"

Plywood has been nailed over sliding doors or maybe French doors, shards of glass and splintered wood barely visible in the darkness. The younger man rattles the kitchen doorknob. Pounds the door with the side of his fist. "Charmaine?"

Gus gasps, "She – she can't be in there."

"She's gone in before."

"She got a key or something?"

"She finds a way in." The younger man studies the back of the house, surveying the windows upstairs and down. Tugs at the plywood sheets.

Gus wonders if the woman is the one who broke the patio sliders. "We should call the cops."

"Look, you know me. You and I've said hello. My wife, she hasn't been well. I've found her in here before, sitting in some corner, crying."

Gus shifts his eyes toward the other man. "Okay, but I'll go in too to make sure you don't take anything."

Sam Martin nods, then strides across the patio, glass crunching under his feet, grabs a tattered lawn chair and positions it below a window at the far end of the house.

Using the chair like a stepladder, he puts a foot on the front of the seat frame and his other foot on the top of the chair back. It wobbles, but holds his weight as he presses the bottom part of the window upward, then hefts himself inside.

Sam looks down at Gus from the open window, says, "I'll let you in the kitchen door so you can keep an eye on me."

He ducks inside and a few seconds later the kitchen door opens. "Can you help me look? If she's not here, I need to get in my car and search the neighborhood. I don't want to waste time."

Gus scurries over. "Is there something wrong with her?"

"No – yes. She's been depressed. If you can look around down here, I'll go upstairs. She's usually up in the nursery." Sam scrapes fingers through his hair.

"The nursery?"

"She miscarried in April. You can bring your dog inside."

Gus shuffles into the kitchen, though he doesn't like it much, breaking into someone else's house. Then it hits him. She was pregnant. Lost a baby. His second wife had lost one too all those years back.

It's musty and dark inside, empty over six months. Mars works for the listing agent and says she wants to sell to someone who'll turn it into a bed and breakfast. Sniffing the stale air, Gus shakes his head. Whoever buys this place has his work cut out for him.

He peeks into the murky living room. Gracie runs her nose along the carpet at his feet. The drapes are open and the streetlights have flicked on outside, casting an eerie atmosphere across the room. What's that by the window, catching the light?

"Hello?" Gus' voice sounds weak and frightened. What's the doc's wife's name? He clears his throat and says "hello" again, moving slowly into the room, cursing his old

238

man eyes. The dog scrambles ahead, pulling the leash taut, and snatches something from the floor. Gus leans down and yanks it from her, a crumpled white bag, stinking of French fries.

Floorboards creak above his head, Gracie yelps, and Gus jumps. "Hell!" Dropping the bag, he hurries out of the room, not quite remembering where the kitchen is, stopping to glance into another room, dark and foreboding, with what he takes for headless shoulders at first glance, his mouth going dry, only to realize what he sees are the vague outlines of dining room chairs.

Back into the hall, peering toward the front door and a staircase, he shouts, "Dr. Martin!"

A thundering down the stairs startles him. The dog lets out two sharp barks. Sam Martin arrives at the bottom, asking, "Did you find her?"

"No. Just an old French fry bag. Maybe it's hers?"

Somewhere in the dark house a sound. Not a slam, but a kind of knocking.

"What was —" asks Gus.

Gracie growls.

Sam hisses. "Shhh!"

Gus leans down and picks her up, clamps her muzzle, just as Sam grabs the older man's shirt and drags him to a door near the kitchen.

Sam whispers, "Wait here," and slowly turns the knob. The door squeaks as it opens. Cool air gusts up. Stairs lead down.

Gus watches the young man descend into the blackness below. Gracie quivers in his arms. Gus takes one or two steps down and leans over to see what he can see. Nothing, so he takes another step. He wishes he had a flashlight.

Below there's a grunt and the crash of glass and metal against cement and something bumps into Gus' forehead knocking him against the wall, Gracie leaping out of his grasp, finding her feet on the stairs, and yapping in hot pursuit. Gus gulps for air, tries to straighten up, feels a hand under his elbow.

"You okay?" asks Sam Martin.

Gus nods and they lumber up the stairs, the dog ranting at a corner of the kitchen. Sam searches for a light switch, flicks it on, but it doesn't work. He opens the door and they hasten out, something following after, Gracie in the doorway, still barking. A full moon glints in the glass scattered across the patio.

"Was that her?" asks Gus, disoriented, breathing hard.

Sam doesn't answer right away. He plops down onto the step, burying his head in his hands. "No. It was a bat."

Hot and light-headed, Gus pivots toward the backyard, and catches in the moonlight, just for a moment, a glimpse of his second wife, the one who lost a baby, the one who never wanted Mars, the son of his first.

# Heat

The oaks and sycamores along the Old Road offer shade, but do nothing to alleviate the oppressive heat. Only when the summer sun falls behind the ridge on the other side of Riolito Creek does Gus tether Gracie and head out. It's that shadowy time of day when his eyes can't pick out the rocks or sticks in his path so he doesn't trek down to the creek, but takes to the sidewalk. He's slow, and so is the dog, both of them old and drained of energy even though they've stayed inside all day in front of an oscillating fan from Walmart.

He smells barbeque, but knows it's not from the cottages or the Trencher mansion or the bungalow where the fake doctor lives. Maybe from the Tudor on the corner, that couple with loud grandchildren who come for a week and raise Cain all over the neighborhood.

"Gus."

He turns at the sound of Sybil's voice. She's behind him on the sidewalk in slacks and shirt and wearing tennis shoes for a change. She's a handsome woman, he thinks, or at least *was*, at some point.

"Aren't you going to the creek today?"

"Too dark. Too damn hot. Don't feel like climbing back up."

"Can I join?"

He shrugs and ambles on, letting her catch up. Gracie trots along looking up at Sybil, waiting to be noticed.

"I see you there, Gracie," says Sybil. "I can't get down there right now to pat your head, but I see you."

They walk in silence past the Tudor – no B-B-Q here – across Portola and south along the Old Road, six or seven houses on the left, all of them in need of paint except for one, glossy with recent attention, and on the right, the creek deep in the arroyo.

Finally Sybil asks, "Have you talked to the young doctor lately?"

"Me?" asks Gus. "Why should I talk to him?" He pictures Sam Martin's face, lined with worry on the night they broke into the Trencher mansion. "He's not a real doctor, you know."

"He is a real doctor, for Pete's sake. And you know him. You went into the Trencher house with him to find his wife."

The man's wife has been missing three weeks. Gus talked to the police, told them everything about that night. Even about the bat that flew out of the basement. And he remembers Sam's face, can't get rid of Sam's face.

"I wish things could go back to the way they were before the storm," he says, "or when the cottages were cabins, when there was trout in the creek."

"Can't live in the past, Gus."

"Am I going to have to move?"

The sudden change in subject startles her. "I'm not selling, I told you that. Actually Ian hasn't bothered me about it lately. Neither has his mother."

"Glad to hear it. Not right to kick someone out of their house."

Sybil looks at him. "It's my house, Gus."

"I pay my rent and on time."

They're coming to the place along the Old Road where it curves up and away from the creek. They turn around and start back toward the cottages, stopping for Gracie to pee and sniff. When they get close to the Martin bungalow, Sybil says, "You should go in and check on the doctor. Make sure he's all right, give him someone to talk to."

"Why would I do that? I don't even know him. Besides, what if he did it? Killed his wife and I go snooping around?"

"Oh, Gus, sometimes." She stops walking. Gus doesn't notice or pretends not to notice and shambles on.

# A Kindness

The next morning, Sybil finds herself on the front porch of the Martin bungalow. Weeds grow around the abandoned ladder in the yard, a stack of wood has been knocked over and scattered, the light above her head still burns.

After a restless, guilt-ridden night, she can't help herself. She only knows the doctor well enough to wave or chat about the weather on the few occasions they've run into each other. But maybe, she thinks, someone from the neighborhood should pay him a visit despite the cloud of suspicion around him. Maybe even *because* of the cloud.

When Gus told her about what happened in the Trencher mansion the day Charmaine disappeared, Sybil's impression was that the doctor had no idea what happened to his wife, that he was desperate to find her. Only after several visits to the bungalow by police and press did Gus begin to say he might have misinterpreted the situation. Now he and everyone else seem to think the podiatrist might have harmed her.

Sybil knocks twice more before the door opens.

"Yes," Sam Martin says, his voice low and disinterested.

"I'm Sybil. I own the cottages next door, and I've been thinking about you and your wife. I don't know if the police told you, but Charmaine is not the only woman on this street to go missing."

"They asked me if they were friends. They weren't."

"How are you holding up?"

"Not well. Would you like to come in?"

Tarps cover the floor. The living room walls are scraped of their wallpaper, the built-in cabinets on either side of the fireplace are sanded down. Paint buckets, tools, stacks of mail are scattered around. He signals Sybil to follow him into the dining room where a small flat-screen TV hangs on the wall opposite a shabby sofa placed beneath a large window. On the coffee table are remnants of a rotisserie chicken still in its plastic container.

"Sorry for the mess," he says. "Please sit." He clears off the table and stuffs everything into an overflowing trashcan in the corner. A Styrofoam cup and a crumpled napkin fall to the floor.

"I'm sorry to barge in on you, Doctor Martin. I didn't know if anyone in the neighborhood had come by to see how you are, and I thought someone should." She hesitates, then asks, "How *are* you?"

He glances around for a chair, but there isn't one, mutters, "Just a minute," and ducks into the kitchen and drags a stool into the dining room and sits down.

"How am I?" He stares at his bare feet, at a pile of newspapers on the floor, up at Sybil. "I think I'm losing my mind."

In her softest voice, she says, "If you want me to leave, I will, but if you want to talk, I'll listen."

And he opens up as if he hasn't talked for a year. He tells her about going into debt to buy the bungalow only to find that everything needed replacement or repair, from the attic to the basement, behind every wall, a new problem. Then the baby was coming and then not coming, and Charmaine, the dreamer, always seeing potential in everything, blind to all downsides until they happened, giving into angry depression. He tells Sybil he's the police's prime suspect. Perhaps, they hint, he accidentally lost his temper and panicked. But he didn't do anything to her. He wouldn't, but she might have done something to herself.

He tells Sybil how Charmaine took a hammer to the new tile in their bathroom, how she lay in bed for days, how she walked for hours along the creek, how he'd look for her, first checking the diner on Portola, the Trencher mansion, the arroyo only to come home and find her in bed, her Xanax bottle on the nightstand. He never knew how many she took, so he dumped them out. That was one of their biggest fights.

Sybil wishes she hadn't come, but glad she did, glad it isn't Gus this man is spilling his heart to.

# Good Deed

He is sweet and gentle toward her, reassuring her that he would never hurt her, that he just needs to keep her with him for a short time – too short – while he deals with some personal issues. Nothing to do with her, really, and he is sorry.

What amazes her is how quickly fear has driven away her lethargy. It happened in an instant. She wants her life back. Wants Sam. Wants to try for another baby. What she doesn't want is this!

The bed is shoved into an area of the basement that was dug out years and years ago to put in a gravity heater. It's a room, away from the stairs, cinderblock to about five feet and then just dirt, a crawlspace about two or three feet high underneath the house. It's black both day and night, all cellar openings around the perimeter of the house covered with plywood. There are lights, though. He turns on the one in the dry-walled storage space when he comes downstairs, but rarely the one in the furnace area.

He apologizes, too, for her nakedness and for the handcuffs around her wrists and ankles. He wishes he could trust her to help him voluntarily, let her do this as a good deed, but he can't. Surely she can understand that and he can't afford anything else to go wrong. Too much has already gone wrong. And time is running out. She can see that, can't she? How he's trying to make it all work before his wife and daughter come home?

The bed is comfortable, the quilt is soft and warm, her pillow eiderdown. The first time he flicked on the light, she was surprised to find that it was a tiny chandelier. The food he brings down to her on real china is plain, but delicious. She tells herself these are good signs. Yet it's his eyes, hard as diamonds, that scare her.

He must know this because he comes to her in the darkness, whispers in her ear how much he loves her, that all he wants to do is stroke her body. He promises only to tease and tweak, stroke and fondle. She should relax and enjoy. Let him cover her with little kisses, gentle caresses, until her pleasure becomes desire, and she wants him, needs him, as much as he needs her.

# Unravelling

Sybil lies naked in her bed, sleeping off Margaritas, her windows open because of the heat, the air as dry as ash, wildfires in the nearby hills sucking up oxygen. The shouts are part of her dream — a dream in which she scrambles down the corridor of a speeding train, children and old men blocking her way. She leaps over dogs, shoves conductors into seats, then finds herself clinging to a window ledge outside the passenger car, sand and wind blasting, mountains hurtling, and all the while, there is yelling, yelling, and now barking ...

She wakes up. The barking doesn't stop. Neither does the yelling, the unfamiliar voices swiftly familiar. Ian Shane from next door and — is that Gus' son, Mars? Of course it is. Ever since Ian's mother and Mars jumped into bed together, the tension between lover and son has crackled every time they meet. Sybil grabs her robe from the floor and glancing at the clock — 1:00 AM — scurries into her living room to peek from behind the curtain.

Light blazes in Ian's bungalow, his windows flung up because of the heat, while Gracie barks in Gus' open doorway as the old man stumbles past her onto his porch. Then, as Sybil watches, Gus tumbles down the steps, landing on his side on the sidewalk. She's out the door, hurrying to him, calling out "Mars! Ian!" as she goes.

Reaching the old man, she stoops down. He groans, "My hip, my hip." Gracie whines and sniffs.

"Is it broken?" Sybil glances over his crumpled body, shouts, "Mars, come help!" The courtyard remains empty, the hollering inside continues. No one is rushing out to help. She glimpses a coyote. The animal, slinking down the middle of the Old Road, turns his head toward her, eyes glinting, before moving on.

"I'm calling an ambulance," she says to Gus. "Do not move."

She straightens – her own bones creaking – and hurries up Ian's steps, pounds once on his door, bursts in.

Ian is rolled into a ball in a corner, arms and hands covering his head. Mars stands over him, fists clenched. She shivers in the hot night air, keeps her voice low, but firm. "Mars, your father's fallen in front of his house. Go outside and see to him while I call an ambulance."

He pivots toward her, his face bewildered, and mumbles. "He's okay. I only hit him once. Not that hard."

"Go take care of your father. Now."

"Dad?"

"He fell. Go." She pushes him toward the door and he goes, reluctantly.

Ian, wearing only boxers, is unfolding on the floor. She leans over him. "Are you hurt? How bad?"

He extends his arms, reddish bruises already beginning to form, his left eye swelling.

"Okay," Sybil says. "Doesn't look too bad. Stay still. Let me call an ambulance for Gus. Where's your cell?"

"In the bedroom. On the nightstand."


In the emergency waiting room, slumped forward in his chair, Mars hides his face in his hands. He's been this way for the better part of an hour. Gus and Ian are beyond the swinging doors and Ian's mother, Rita, is on her way. Sybil tightens the raincoat she snatched from her closet before driving Mars to the hospital.

"They'll be all right," she reassures him.

Ian's wounds appear superficial, but they're checking for internal bleeding. Sybil doesn't know about Gus. Broken hips often lead to decline in older people, she thinks, forgetting that Gus isn't all that much older than she is.

The door from outside whooshes open and in storms Rita, hair almost perfect, sweatpants immaculate, lugging her designer handbag.

"Mrs. Shane." Sybil pulls herself up in her chair, but the woman marches past her, over to Mars, and kicks him in the shin, and as he straightens, she slaps his cheek.

Rita leans over, taking advantage of his sitting position, spit coming out with every word. "That's my son in there and no one beats up my son. Do you *hear* me, you stupid piece of crap?"

Mars doesn't move. Says quietly, "He accused me of kidnapping that woman, the one that's missing. He said you said it was true." He raises his head and stares at Rita.

"So you beat him up?"

"I lost my temper."

"That's what people like you do, and don't you think it's a little coincidental that you show up and two women disappear?"

When Sybil rises, Rita turns on her. "*You* stay out of my way."

A security guard appears and Rita shakes him off too, holds up her hands to show she's done and moves three or four steps back. "Just take me to see my son."


After they're gone, Sybil says gently, "Mars? Are you okay?" He doesn't answer, but lifts himself from his chair and moves trance-like across the waiting room and through the door into the night.

Sybil considers going after him, but hesitates. Could he have anything to do with the disappearances? Jamie's? Charmaine's? She doesn't believe it. She knows men. She understands Mars.

A doctor – Sybil can tell by his confident stride – comes out of the emergency room and says to Sybil, "Are you Mrs. German?"

"No, I'm not." She stands up, holds out her hand. "I'm Gus' landlady and a friend."

"What happened to his son?"

"Oh. He went out for some air. Is Gus going to be all right? Did he break his hip?"

"I need to talk to a member of the family."

"Okay, I'll see if I can find him, but Gus is okay, isn't he?"

The doctor's mouth is an impatient frown. "Let the nurse know when he shows," then quickly disappears behind the double doors.

Exhaustion takes Sybil by surprise and she sinks back into her chair. She should go get Mars, but her mind wanders to Jamie, instead. If Jamie were here, I wouldn't be alone. We could help Gus together, two women of strength, getting through this difficult year. And help sort out Mars.

There are other things, too, she would explain to Jamie if she was here. About men. Most men. And about women like Rita Shane. How they tumble through life blinded to the faintest outlines of love and kindness, self-worth and contentment. And what good is having earned wisdom if there's no one to listen? The windstorm that blew through the Old Road toppled more than just trees. If Jamie were only here, Sybil is sure she'd find the strength to move, to go

252

find Mars, keep him and his father from combusting in each other's presence.

Then other "ifs" force themselves on her, so many through the years, but one that presses her now.

That baby she had when she was sixteen. Dale's baby. She begged her grandpa to let her stay with him after the summer ended, not make her go back to her Catholic parents who would send her to a nunnery with other bad girls, and put the baby up for adoption. But he refused, and when her little girl was born, she was taken away. And now, Sybil is left with no one. Not even the blue jay.

I need to find Mars German and drag him back.

I will do that.

In a minute.

She breathes in and out.

In and out.

# Devil Wind

It happens every October. Hot Santa Ana winds whip through Southern California, day and night, stripping leaves from oaks, sucking up moisture. The devil stokes his furnace, and heat rises from the ground.

Sybil scuffs through her cottage, muttering, "I don't feel like myself. I don't know what's wrong with me." She shakes her head as she moves through her darkened living room into the brightness of the kitchen. She blinks and turns back into the shadows. She feels old, older than she's ever felt before. She stops at the window and stares into the courtyard. It's too much. Too much.

She imagines Gus in his cottage, TV on, Gracie on his lap, his mind wandering from his aching fake hip to the naked branches outside, to his son's homelessness. The operation was successful, but painful, his walks with the dog now confined to the yellowing courtyard, a ramp to accommodate his walker. The rotating fan drones on.

She suspects that next door Ian is sprawled on his bathroom floor having spent most of the previous night with old high school friends – laughing, drinking and music so loud she had to bang on his door and threaten to call the police.

Across the courtyard, Mrs. Renke's bungalow is coffin-dry, empty six months now, her belongings collected by son and granddaughter, the left-overs donated to the Salvation Army. The few boxes stacked in the dining area belong to Jamie for when she returns with her two small children.

Rent money is less important to her than Jamie and the kids having a place to come back to.

Back to the bedroom, she sprawls across the bed. So tired. So tired.

"Sybil?" Someone outside is calling her name. She didn't realize she'd fallen asleep. The voice comes again. Louder and closer to her bedroom window.

It's Gus.

She doesn't want to talk to Gus, but the landlady part of her — what if it's a gas leak? — forces her up. She peeks out the bedroom window and sees Gus moving slowly along the side of her cottage toward the front, gripping his walker, Gracie's leash tangled around one of its legs. She raps on the window but he doesn't hear.

Retying the sash of her robe, Sybil scurries through her living room. The heat hits her when she opens the front door, the wind quiet for the moment, the bitter scent of smoke drifting in. Must be a fire in the hills nearby.

Gus clumps around the corner of her porch, sweat trickling down his face. "You okay?" he asks, poking his wrinkled face toward Sybil, squinting, his breathing hard.

"I'm okay, Gus. What about you? What are you doing?" She holds onto the door, tries to keep annoyance out of her voice.

"You didn't answer my knock. Thought maybe you fell."

"I'm all right, Gus. You shouldn't be back there in all that dirt with your walker. Look," she says coming down the steps, "Gracie's all snarled up."

"Don't I know it? I hate this damn thing."

"Are you doing your PT?" she asks unwrapping the leash.

"That doesn't do any good."

"What can I do for you, Gus?"

"Mars could fix your sprinklers. He could use the work."

She eyes the old man. "Haven't seen him around lately. Where's he staying?"

"Don't know. Maybe down at the Soup Kitchen."

"Come on in. If you hold onto me and the railing, you should be able to get up the steps. I'll make us some ice tea."

"I don't like ice tea much."

"Come in anyway," she says impatiently and points him toward the couch, adding, "Change of scenery will do you good."

He drops onto the cushions with a grunt, sweat trickling down his forehead.

"You want some water?"

"Coffee'd be fine."

"Coffee? On a day like this?"

"I like coffee." He leans back, Gracie curling in his lap, and closes his eyes.

"Okay," she mutters. "Instant."

When she comes back with a cup of coffee in one hand and ice tea in the other, she asks, "That's okay with you if he's living at a shelter?"

Gus opens his eyes. "He's done it before."

"Yet you're over here finding him work."

"Work's one thing. Charity's another." The old man's voice rises. "I don't want him living with me."

"Don't yell. You're scaring your dog." This isn't true, but it has the right effect on Gus.

The lethargy she's felt all day dissipates a little as Sybil opens the shades. She glances through the glass into the courtyard and sees that the sprinklers must not be working. Odd that Gus would even notice.

"I just don't know, Sybil. Just don't know anymore."

She swipes her daily paper off an armchair and sits down, puts her feet up on the footrest. "What don't you know? Why couldn't he live with you? You have two bedrooms over there."

"He's a grown man."

"So what?"

Gus frowns. "The police think he killed that woman. They talked to him. That's what that fight was about. Ian telling Mars that Rita kicked him out because she thought he snatched that Charmaine."

"If cops thought that, he'd be in jail."

"He's been in jail before."

"For murder?"

"No, nothing like that."

"Rita said all that because she wanted to get rid of Mars. Isn't that new boyfriend, that investment banker, ten years younger than her?"

"My son, Sybil, he's just no good."

"Gus," she says sharply. "You can't blame everything on Mars. Why are you so hard on him?"

"He made life hell for my second wife and she made life hell for me."

"You gotta let that go."

"I'm too old."

"You're too lazy. You need him now anyway. A new hip. Having him stay with you would help out with the rent. Mars can pay his share by doing stuff around here, and you can pay half of what you do now."

"I've earned my peace."

Sybil presses fingers to her forehead and rubs hard. So amazing to her that Gus can love that dog like he does and not have one good thought about his own son.

They sit for a while longer, not talking, the heavy day pressing down.

Finally Sybil leans forward. "How do you reach Mars? Does he have a phone?"

"He comes for Mac-and-Cheese every once in a while."

Sybil bites her tongue. If she had the energy, she'd take the old fart by the shoulders and tell him to take care of his son. Instead, she says, "Tell him I need him to do some work when he comes."

"If he shows up."

# Changes

Mars slicks back his hair, damp from his shower, checks the thoroughness of his shave in the mirror, straightens his frayed denim shirt. Not bad, he thinks. The best he can do in a place like this. He misses Rita. At least, he misses her house, her swimming pool, her bed. He grimaces, shakes his head. Better get going.

He strides out of First Light Mission into the bracing air and turns south. Cars rumble along the parkway, an old Beastie Boys song pounding from someone's radio. Mars lifts his chin. Beneath a cloudless sky, the peaks of distant mountains gleam with first snow. The song he just heard repeats in his head. "You gotta fight for the right ..." He grins. With Thanksgiving less than a week away, there should be plenty of work.

"Hey, man. Slow down."

Mars pivots, and waits as a short, solid man trots to catch up.

"Javi," says Mars. "How's that bambino?"

The other man rolls his eyes. "*En español es 'bebé'*. No sleep. Nada. My wife is, uh, *es como una pantera*. Walking, how you say, how you say — when you walk up and down, up and down?"

"You mean, pacing? She's worried?"

"Yes, yes. She worry. She tired. No sleep. No money. No happy."

"Well," says Mars, slapping Javi on the back, "then we'd better get at it."

Three blocks down, a group of laborers mill in front of the Home Depot, some sitting on a low cinderblock wall, drinking coffee, others smoking, kidding around, a few approaching pick-up trucks as they turn into the parking lot. A couple of guys linger across the street in front of the U-Haul, although a Wednesday in the middle of the month isn't prime moving time. The best jobs come from contractors and do-it-yourselfers, especially if a worker can hang drywall, lay brick, install a laminate floor. Mars can do all these jobs and hopes someone will take him on as a regular, at least through the holidays.

An Escalade slows to the curb, and Mars and Javi look up expectantly. The passenger window hums down and the woman behind the wheel leans across the seat, takes off her sunglasses, and smiles at Mars. "I need someone to remove some wallpaper?"

Mars puts a hand on the window frame, smiles back. He wonders if she's a realtor like Rita or maybe a house flipper.

Javi pipes up, "I can do that. Real good, real fast, real cheap."

She's still eyeing Mars. "Are you real cheap too?"

Mars backs away, glances at Javi. "This young man's the best you can get and very reasonable for the quality of his work."

Her lips part in surprise, her head tilts, and then she turns to Javi. "How much?"

"Only eight dollars an hour."

"Ten and he's a steal." Mars nods at her, and she nods back.

"Okay, Mr. Ten-Dollars-an-Hour. Hop in." And Javi does just that.

Mars watches the SUV speed away just as another car, strapped with an empty trailer, bumps from the U-Haul lot over the curb into the street and up the Home Depot driveway, sending men scrambling.

"What the hell!" shouts Mars.

He recognizes the driver, Ian Shane, at the same time Ian Shane recognizes him, and jumps out of the way thinking, Rita's son plans to run me down.

But the car and trailer screech to a stop and Ian starts laughing. "You should see your face. Like I'd try to take you on."

"What just happened?" Mars opens Ian's car door. The laborers bunch up around them.

Ian shrugs. "Saw you when I was getting the trailer, and I wasn't paying attention when I headed this way. You want some work?"

"What kind of work? Not with your mother."

"She's gone. You wanna help me move?"

"What do you mean, she's gone?"

"Get in and I'll tell you all about it."

Even if this is a trick, Mars knows Ian Shane is no threat. Gus calls him the shiny penny, the mama's boy. Mars says, "You'd better let me drive."

Once they're on their way, Ian says, "She cut me off, you know. Fired me, stopped paying my rent. Took off with some dude to Bali."

"I thought she was going to get rich on the Old Road development."

"Dead in the water."

They become silent, Ian grinding his teeth, Mars smirking as they pass a row of half-demolished 1950's apartment buildings.

"Hey, listen, I'm sorry she gave your name to the police. Sorry I had anything to do with it."

"Sorry I went after you. It's just when you said she said that, I lost it. It was so out of left field."

"I get it. I've had to deal with her my whole life."

They drive for a while, the empty trailer clattering behind them. Then Ian says, "That was crazy all of us at the hospital in the middle of the night. Your dad seems to be doing all right."

"I guess. I don't see him much."

Turning onto the Old Road, Mars asks, "So where you moving to?"

"In with a friend. He's got a condo downtown."

"What are you gonna do, you know, for money?"

"Real estate. It's what I know. It's what she taught me. I just didn't realize she'd screw me over like she does everyone else."

# News

On the creek side of the Old Road, the sun dips behind the wild growth of the arroyo and hills beyond, cooling the warm California afternoon. Mars sits on his dad's porch, shuffling cards, first overhand three or four times, then open face, then riffling them in an arc before letting them cascade.

"You gonna deal those things?" asks Gus, his voice gruff, patting the dog on his lap.

"I've got martinis!" Sybil hollers as she emerges from her own cottage.

Mars twists in his chair. "Martinis?"

Gus mumbles under his breath, and Gracie perks her head.

"I know, they're not very Thanksgiving-y, but it's so warm." Sybil moves carefully down her front stairs and starts across the courtyard. She's wearing one of her sarongs, its slit up the side not quite high enough to allow for anything but geisha-girl steps. Mars puts down the cards and hurries to help, taking the loaded tray from Sybil when he reaches her.

"So what are you guys playing?"

"Nothing at the moment. Mr. Las Vegas and all his shuffling," says Gus.

"Gin Rummy," answers Mars. "Take my chair, Sybil." He picks up the deck of cards and puts it on the tray, then puts the tray on the table. Passes out the cocktails, remains standing. "But now that you're here, I have an announcement."

Sybil and Gus exchange a glance. Mars holds up his glass. "Ian Shane and I are flipping a house over on the Northside."

Sybil's eyebrows shoot up.

Gus says, "With whose money?"

"Ian's. I guess he's been squirreling away his money since he first started working. This'll be his project, but I'm the contractor. And I'm staying there while we fix it up."

"It'll never work."

"Oh, Gus, drink your drink. Congratulations, Mars. Maybe things are finally taking a turn for the better." As soon as she says the words, they feel like wishful thinking, something that's never worked for her. She sips the margarita, tastes salt.

Gracie barks.

A man and a woman slam car doors. Stride into the courtyard. Mars shakes his head and plops down on the steps.

They're almost to the porch before Sybil recognizes them as the two detectives, the woman again in black, the man this time wearing a windbreaker, who spoke to her about Jamie's disappearance.

"All we want to do is to find out if anyone has heard from Jamie or Joel Prentiss?" says Detective Hierra.

Sybil shakes her head. "Nothing at all. Did you ever find any relatives?"

Detective Ross answers, "An aunt in Oregon, but she hasn't heard anything. Seems Jamie and the kids don't want to be found."

"Or can't be found," says Sybil, her eyes welling up.

# A Distant Star

They bury her on Saturday morning, the sky a misty shroud. The family sits in a neat row next to the grave. Mother and father in black, and of course her husband, and next to him, his family in navy and gray except for the sister-in-law in a blue print, a baby wriggling in her arms. Friends, about thirty of them surround this tableau, a few chairs near the front for older mourners like Gus. Mars and Sybil hover nearby.

Sybil begins to tremble as she remembers the day the detectives told them how the body was found. It was Ross, the woman, who spoke in a soft, but matter-of-fact voice. A teenage girl was thrown from her horse while riding up by the Homestead Dam. She wasn't hurt. She landed on soft sand and though the wind was knocked out of her, she laughed because falling off a horse is something that happens, but the horse wouldn't come back for her. Every time she called him, he'd take a step forward, then step back, and snort.

At one point, Gus had interrupted the detective, telling him to get on with it and for once, Sybil appreciated the old man's impatience. Ross didn't notice and kept talking.

The girl pulled herself up, brushed off the dirt and weeds, and looked for her hat. She stepped beyond the tall grass and saw a mound of dirt and a hole dug up by a dog or coyote. She tiptoed closer and for a few seconds, she wasn't sure what she saw. As she adjusted her eyes, she recognized two bones, the curve of an arm.

Now Charmaine is being laid into the ground again. The minister finishes his commentary, and a woman, her best friend, tells how close she and Charmaine had always been, and then it's Sam's turn.

"This is Rilke," he says. "One of – one of Charmaine's favorites. It's called 'Lament.'" He stares at a piece of paper in his shaking hands, reads:

Oh! All things are long passed away and far.
A light is shining but the distant star
From which it still comes to me has been dead
A thousand years ... In the dim phantom boat
That glided past some ghastly thing was said.
A clock just struck within some house remote.
Which house? – I long to still my beating heart.
Beneath the sky's vast dome I long to pray ...
Of all the stars there must be far away
A single star which still exists apart.
And I believe that I should know the one
Which has alone endured and which alone
Like a white City that all space commands
At the ray's end in the high heaven stands.

Silence follows as Sam breaks off in a sob.

Sybil glances around the gathering. She recognizes the chef from the Portola diner wearing a dark suit, hands clasped in front of him, and the man next to him looks familiar too. He's stepping away from the crowd. She can't place him, but he's staring at her, or maybe beyond her.

Sybil turns and sees Ian plodding up the little hill toward the gravesite. He's wearing casual clothing, as if he hadn't meant to come. Then right behind him comes a little girl and a little boy holding hands with a woman. Jamie! Sybil gasps, totters. Mars grabs her arm and follows her gaze.

Collin breaks into a run and throws himself at Sybil. She grabs hold of him. And then they are all there. Shushing each other.

"Have some respect." It's Gus' harsh whisper that quiets them down. They turn and watch the rest of the ceremony, Jamie clasping Sybil's hand, squeezing it, and Sybil squeezing back.

When it's over, after they've each thrown a white flower onto the coffin, the little group from the cottages begins to wander back down the hill.

In whispers, Jamie and Sybil talk and squeeze each other's hands again.

"Oh, sweet girl," says Sybil. "Where have you been?"

Jamie shakes her head. "We went to Canada – Vancouver. A friend from high school lives there. I wanted to give Joel time to start a new life."

"And did he?"

"He did. He wants to get married, so we're getting a divorce."

"And that's what you want?" asks Sybil softly.

"It's a start." Jamie squeezes Sybil's hand. "You've been so good to me. You're like a mom, Sybil, and I hope you'll forgive me for not calling. I was just afraid –"

Sybil shakes her head. "Nothing to forgive."

"Oh, look," says Jamie, "There's my old psychology teacher."

Everyone turns to watch the man who is watching them, eyes settling on Jamie.

# Recognition

'Appendages', Pushcart Nomination, *Atticus Review*, 2013

'Between Hay and Grass, 1949', Finalist, 2013,
   *Bosque* Fiction Prize

'Beyond the Curve', Winner, 2008/2009 Winter Flash
   Contest at *Women on Writing*

'Heaven Spoils', Finalist, 2015 *Lascaux* Prize in Flash Fiction

'Kindling', 4th Place, 2013 AWP Heat Contest

'Losing Ground', Monthly Contest Winner,
   *Tattoo Highway, 2009*

'Mischief', 23rd Place, 13th Annual *Writer's Digest*
   Short-Short Story Competition, 2013

'Monsoon', Finalist, Winter 2007-2008 *Glimmer Train*
   Fiction Open

'Oranges', Pushcart Nomination, *Every Day Fiction*, 2011

'Small Town', Honorable Mention, July 2013 Very Short
   Fiction Award *Glimmer Train*

'Something about L.A.', Winner, The Eleventh Glass
   Woman Prize

'Spring Melt', Pushcart Nomination, *Every Day Fiction*,
   2008 and Micro Award, Finalist, 2009

'What's Left', Honoree, 2010 Ultra-Short Contest,
   *The Binnacle*

'Wounded Moon', Short-listed, Fish Short Story Prize, 2009

# Previously Published

'200 Nights', *Corium*
'6 A.M.', *Emprise Review*
'Abbreviated Glossary', *Melusine*
'Appendages', *Atticus Review*
'Between Hay and Grass, 1949', *Bosque (The Magazine)*
'Beyond the Curve', *Women on Writing*
'Blusterfuck', *Pure Slush*
'Body-Snatching', *LITnIMAGE*
'Broke and Broken', *50 to 1*
'Chalk Dust', *Night Train Magazine*
'Complicit', *SmokeLong Quarterly*
'Cords', *SmokeLong Quarterly*
'Doing Mr. Velvet', *The Battered Suitcase*
'Eye for an Eye', *Right Hand Pointing*
'Flash Flood', *Every Day Fiction*
'Gumbo', *JMWW*
'Isla Vista, 1970', *Foundling Review*
'Jericho Beach', *Stripped, A Collection of Anonymous Flash*
'Kindling', *Prime Number*
'Last Four Songs', *Pure Slush*
'Losing Ground', *Tattoo Highway*
'Mischief', 13th Annual *Writer's Digest* Short Short
    Story Publication
'Monsoon', *Women's Quality Fiction*
'Oranges', *Every Day Fiction*
'Pomegranate', *Pomegranate Stories*
'Ruby', *decomP Magazine*

'Running the Fence', *Monkeybicycle*
'Sediment', *Blue Five Notebook*
'She Can't Say No', *Paradigm Journal*
'Small Town', *Metazen*
'Something About L.A.', *Litsnack*
'Spring Melt', *Every Day Fiction*
'The Last Real Human Being in Hollywood', *Pure Slush*
'The Real War', *Clapboard House*
'The Way It Can Be', *Dogzplot*
'Tools of the Trade', *Writers' Bloc (Rutgers)*
'What's Left', *The Binnacle Magazine*
'Wounded Moon', *Short Story America Anthology, Vol. I*

Versions of some chapters in *The Old Road* originally
published as part of *2014 A Year in Stories* by Pure Slush
Books, 2013 – 2014.

# About the Author

Gay Degani began writing in the fifth grade and placed second in the *Atlantic Monthly Writing Contest for High School Students* when she was a high school senior. She followed this surprising honor with a twenty-five-year hiatus from her typewriter, turning her attention to college, career, and family. With the help of a computer, she began again in 1999. Her short stories have been published online and in print. Three have been nominated for Pushcart consideration while a few others have placed first or been recognized in competitions. Her suspense novel, *What Came Before*, was published in 2014, preceded by an eight-story collection, *Pomegranate Stories*, in 2010. She is the founder and editor emeritus at *Flash Fiction Chronicles*, an editor at *Smoke-Long Quarterly*, and blogs at *Words in Place*.

Author photograph © Ed Danes